King of the Streets, Queen of His Heart 3

A Legendary Love Story

PORSCHA STERLING

They struggle...

Meet Quentin

QUENTIN

"**P**ops, please...I can't do that shit. Please don't make me do that!" Quentin pleaded with his father as he stared at his hard, stone-cold face, his narrowed eyes laced with his evil intentions.

"SHUDDUP!" Gene demanded in a loud whisper. "You're gonna do it and you're gonna do it tonight or else you know what I'm gonna do to you!"

Quentin shuddered and his bottom lip began to quiver as he thought about the meaning behind his father's words.

When Gene returned home from prison, no one was happier than Quentin to know that his father was returning home. The only problem was Leith, Sr., who had told Monice that it was a bad idea to take the boys to see him. After pleading to see his father over and over again, Quentin was ecstatic when she finally agreed to sneak him to see Gene as much as she could.

During those meetings, Gene seemed like the father that Quentin had always saw him as. He referred to Quentin as "his good son" and told *him that he wasn't a traitor like the others. For once, Quentin felt like he wasn't being treated like an outsider...like someone truly wanted him. Although he had four brothers, none of them seemed to really like him. Not even his own twin, Quan.*

When Gene moved in and reclaimed his place as 'head nigga in charge' after Leith Sr.'s untimely demise, things began to change. Quentin began to learn what being the 'good son' meant. Prison had really terrorized Gene's mind and, in turn, he terrorized his own son whenever he got the chance, forcing Quentin to acquiesce to his twisted sexual pleasures.

Although Gene physically and verbally abused Leith Jr. and Pablo, Quentin couldn't ever bring himself to feel sorry for them. The punishment they endured was mild in comparison to the violations that he suffered for being his father's favorite son. The hatred in his heart grew each day he saw Leith cry and whimper after being attacked by Gene in a way that, in his mind, was far milder than what he'd had to suffer through.

Looking up at his father, tears came to Quentin's eyes as he realized that there was no way out of his current situation. Gene had given him the ultimatum. It was either him or Crystal. Gene felt like it was time that Cush received her punishment for being a child his beloved Monice had birthed after she'd vowed herself to him while he was locked up, but he knew that he couldn't do it himself.

Monice watched him like a hawk when it came to Crystal. She could see the lustful look in his eyes whenever he saw young Crystal walking around the house, so she made sure to never leave her alone with him and to always keep her eye on her daughter.

She had no idea that she should have also been protecting her sons.

"Go in there and do what I told you," Gene whispered in the dimly lit room. "Give that bitch what she deserves. Daddy will be watchin'."

Tears fell down Quentin's cheek but he quickly brushed them away when he saw Gene's fist ball up. In Gene's household, crying was a felony that would receive a severe and painful sentence.

"Be the good son that I know you are," Gene pushed. "If you do like I tell you, I'll take it easy on you from now on. She deserves it anyways… don't feel sorry for that bitch."

Casting one last doubtful look at the demonic glare on Gene's face, Quentin nodded his head and turned away to walk towards Crystal's room. She was the only girl so she was the only one privileged to have a room to herself. He walked to the door and peered inside. Crystal was sleeping soundly and peacefully. His heart thumped in his chest as he thought about what he had to do.

"Go ahead…I'll be watchin'," Gene's voice said from behind him.

Quentin turned around and watched as Gene walked into the room that Quan and Quentin shared which was right on the other side of Crystal's. Confused, he peeked into Crystal's room and looked at the wall. That's when he noticed, for the first time, a tiny hole in the wall. A hole that Gene was using as his way to witness the assault.

Swallowing hard, Quentin walked into the room slowly and prepared himself for what he had to do. Ripping the covers off of Crystal woke her up instantly.

"Quentin! What are you—"

"Shhh!" he said, roughly covering her mouth with his hand. "Shut da fuck up before you get us both in trouble!"

The horrified look on her face only infuriated him all the more. He didn't want to hurt his sister the way that Gene hurt him but, at the same time, he couldn't help but feeling like Gene was right. If she didn't exist, maybe Gene wouldn't have come home so mad. If Monice had never met Leith Sr., maybe none of the abuse would have ever occurred. It was all of their fault.

Closing his eyes, Quentin tried as hard as he could to squash out his fears and focus on his anger. He needed to in order to do what he had to do because Gene had made it very clear that, if he failed, he would be next.

The car ran over a bump in the road, pulling me from out of my flashback right at the perfect moment. I was out of my medication and had already spent up all my money so there wasn't shit I could do about it.

After leaving prison, I didn't have a thing to my name because the niggas I'd worked with had robbed my ass as soon as they got word that I was locked up. Now here I was, praying that the family I'd once had would help a nigga out. In my heart of hearts, I knew that shit wasn't gonna happen. Even if I could get Quan to listen to me, Murk, Dame, and Legend weren't gonna help me with shit.

I knew that Legend wanted to kill me and he wouldn't hesitate to do it, so the only choice I had was to handle things the way I was about to and hope that it worked. But the longer I went without my meds, the more I could feel myself beginning to change. My pops had awakened a demon in me and it was impossible to control on my own.

"How much fuckin' longer we got to go?!" I asked roughly as I pushed the metal bar into the chick's neck.

She was just as naïve as she looked. All I did was press the bar against the base of her neck and make a clicking noise using a metal pin that I'd made and she was shaking like a leaf thinking I had a gun. I knew too much about my brother to do some shit like that. It would be an immediate death sentence. Shit, showing my fuckin' face might be an immediate death sentence, but I needed to buy some time to try to explain.

"I—it—it's just around the corner here," she answered. Her eyes went to my face through the rearview mirror and for a few minutes, we locked eyes.

Shit, she is fuckin' beautiful, I couldn't help thinking.

Before I could stop myself, my mind instantly traveled to a dark place, and I began to imagine myself doing a few things to her that got my dick rock hard. My eyes cut to the side of the road where there was a small grassy area with a few trees and what appeared to be a small abandoned house. Licking my lips, I toyed with the idea of making her pull over so that I could bring my fantasy to life.

Stop, a voice in my head said suddenly. It was the voice of reason.

Coming to my senses, I shook the dark, lust-filled thoughts away. I brought my closed fist up and pressed it against my temples. These thoughts were fucking with me and if I didn't do something about them, I would find myself in another fucked up situation.

"Here we are," she told me.

Looking up, I could see her eyes were still on me but they were softer, almost like she saw that I was being tortured by my mind. She wasn't as dumb as she looked. Maybe wasn't street-wise but I could see why Legend dealt with her.

"Ease in slowly and don't get out the fuckin' car until I tell you to," I warned, pushing the metal bar further into the nape of her neck.

"Okay," she quietly agreed and bit her lip.

We turned into a gate and she drove in slowly, as I'd instructed. My eyes cut to the front and I saw all four of my brothers standing upfront waiting for me to arrive. They each were already holding their weapons out as if they knew their long-lost brother had returned. I removed the bar from the chick's neck and smiled.

What a sweet welcome home.

"Marisol!" I yelled as I beat on the door to her room. "I'm about to go!"

Seconds later, the door snatched open, revealing Marisol dressed in a worn silk kimono with a long cigarette pulled between her thin lips. She blew the smoke in my face and I jumped back, gagging. The material on her gown was so tattered that one of her nipples showed through as she held it closed with her thin, needle-like fingers. Behind her, a naked man lay sprawled out on the bed as if he owned the place, his flaccid pole resting on the side of his thigh. He grinned and licked his lips as he stared lustfully at me, making me frown. But this wasn't anything new to me. Being the child of a whore, I saw this type of thing all the time.

Chapter One

SHANECIA

I pulled up to the house, thankful that I'd actually managed to make it. I was shaking so badly it was a wonder I could even drive. The entire ride, Quentin hadn't said too much to me after instructing me on where to go, but there was something strange about him. I could see it in his eyes. He was involved in a mental battle, like he was being tortured by his own thoughts. Combine that with the wild and crazy look in his eyes, and I knew this muthafucka was all kinds of insane.

Although the gun was no longer placed at the base of my neck, there was no reason for it to be. I was scared shitless. Even more so than I'd even been when I was taken by Mello. I was high then and was stuck in a place somewhere between a horrible reality and a beautiful dream.

This time, I was aware of every terrifying thing.

Legend, Murk, Dame, and Quan were already standing outside waiting when I pulled into the driveway. A deep frown was implanted on Legend's face as he watched me roll to a stop. After noting that I was unharmed, his eyes fixated on the dark figure behind me and I saw a shadow move behind his eyes. Within seconds, his gun was in the air and he was walking forward as he held it out in front of him.

"GET THE FUCK OUT THE MUTHAFUCKIN' CAR!" he commanded as he crept closer with his gun pointed.

All, except Quan, who wore a stunned expression on his face, followed his lead and pulled up their weapons, aiming it at the car. I tried to duck down to hide from being an accidental target, but Quentin had other plans.

"Naw, baby girl, ain't no time for that shit. I need you," Quentin said in a silky tone that made me sick to my stomach.

He snaked his arm around my neck and pulled me back through the middle console and into the back seat where he sat. My body was pressed up against his and he seemed to enjoy it a little too much, as his hot breath ran across the back of my neck. He smelled like old, hot fish. Disgusting.

"Open the door," he instructed. I did as I was told, keeping my eyes on Legend the entire time. I could see that he was searching for a way to shoot without risking my life. His jaw was clenching and unclenching in frustration the more that he watched. He was frustrated.

Quentin pulled me out of the car and stood behind me, using my body as a shield between himself and the three men holding out weapons in front of me. Quan staggered forward, his eyes still wide as he looked at his brother, the twin that I never knew he had.

"Qu—Quentin, what the fuck are you doin'?" Quan asked him. "Let her go! This ain't you, man."

"Da fuck you mean, 'this ain't him', Quan?" Dame thundered.

"This fuck nigga raped his own fuckin' sister! You forgot what da fuck he did to Cush?"

I felt my heart begin to thump and tears came to my eyes as I thought about Cush's words the other day. I had a feeling that her brother had done something horrible to her, but I'd hoped that wasn't it.

"I didn't want to do that shit to her!" Quentin yelled. "Gene made me do it!"

"Nigga, shut the fuck up!" Legend yelled out through clenched teeth. He squeezed his gun even harder and raised it higher, making Quentin pull me tighter against his body.

"Own up to that shit you did and take your payment like a fuckin' man! Gene ain't make you do shit!" Murk said as he walked to the side opposite of Legend, both of them trying to trap Quentin in the middle as they searched for a way to shoot him without harming me.

"I didn't want to do that shit to Cush, y'all gotta believe me," Quentin said, his voice wavering in a way that caught me off-guard. I peeked at him out the side of my eyes, but he clutched me tighter when he sensed my movement.

"Gene was doin' that shit to me! What he almost did to Legend…I was the one that he was doin' it to. He told me that the only way he would stop is if I obeyed him and did what he told me to do with Cush. There was a hole in the wall in me and Quan's room and he would watch to make sure I did it. I had no fuckin' choice."

Fresh tears came to my eyes but this time it was for Quentin. Although I was still disgusted by the fact that he'd assaulted his sister, the devastation in his voice as he spoke about what his father had done to him was heartbreaking. But, even more so than that, I was shocked by him saying that his father had tried to do the same to Legend.

Slowly, Legend's hardened eyes went from Quentin's face to mine and I could see the vulnerability in them. For a half a second, his expression changed and it nearly mirrored the devastation that could be felt in Quentin's voice. It was true. Quentin's father had tried to rape him when he was younger. That was a secret he'd been keeping from me.

"That still don't pardon you, nigga," Murk spoke up. "Fuck what Gene was tellin' you to do, you still did that shit. You bitch ass nigga."

"Quentin, let her go," Quan said, stepping forward in front of Legend, Murk, and Dame. "This ain't you, man. She's family."

"If Gene is the one who sent you after Cush, then why da fuck you still been followin' her?" Legend asked. "She said she saw you in New York. What your creepy ass was doin' up there?"

Quentin's grip relaxed on me somewhat as he prepared to answer, and I tried to catch Legend's eye to let him know I was about to try to make a move. But, now that Quentin had revealed his secret, he seemed to be trying to avoid my stare as much as possible.

"While I was in lock up, I heard about what y'all niggas was out here doin'. It's easy to get info on the inside. That nigga Mello that y'all fuckin' with? Well, after y'all pushed him out, he had to start movin' weight through some of the prisons to get his cake back up. A little before I was released, I got word that Mello's team had found out the D-Boys had a sister and was gonna use her to get to y'all niggas. As soon as I got out, I checked on her and made sure she saw me because I knew she would tell you."

Cush's words from a few days back came to my mind.

"Legend, I called you to tell you about it, but since you were on a trip with your boo-thang, you ain't wanna listen..."

"And the other night...when you opened a window and climbed up in her spot? What was that about?"

"What?!" Quentin quipped, relaxing his grip on me even more. I moved slightly and he absentmindedly clutched me harder.

"I ain't slipped through no fuckin' window!" Quentin yelled. "I've been here for weeks. After I showed myself to her, I knew she would tell you and you'd get her. I flew down here and heard you had a chick and followed her one day. I was gonna grab her ass the first time I saw her, but she had some light-skinned bitch with her. If someone came in through Cush's window, that was some other shit."

That was Maliah, I thought to myself as my mind went back to the first day I'd seen Quentin when I went to visit the college. *He's right. He's been here for weeks.*

"Da fuck you wanna grab Neesy for?" Dame asked the question I also wanted to know.

"Because if I just walked up on y'all, nigga, Legend would've killed my ass instantly."

"Damn right," Legend affirmed with a tacit nod.

"Listen...I ain't tryna be on no fuck shit. I just need—"

Pow!

11

Before I could even register what was happening, Quan fired off a shot at Quentin's upper leg and grabbed me by my arm, pulling me forward as soon as Quentin released his grip. Legend and Murk charged forward with their weapons out and Quan pushed me to the side as he ran towards them.

Murk gritted his teeth and prepared to pull his trigger as he aimed right at Quentin's head. Blood was oozing from Quentin's upper thigh as he winced and grimaced in pain. He clutched at the wound, blood seeping through his fingers, but he would not cry out.

"Noooo!" Quan yelled, batting Murk's arm out of the way just in time.

Pow!

Murk's gun fired a shot in the opposite direction, nearly hitting Legend in the foot.

"Quan…What the fuck?!" Legend yelled.

"Don't kill him! He's our brother," Quan pled, his brows knotted with distress.

"I don't give a fuck!" Murk and Legend both said at the same time.

"This nigga raped Cush and he's responsible for mama's death! He killed and tortured an entire family. How the hell this nigga ain't get locked up for life, I don't even fuckin' know, but it's okay because now I got the opportunity to end his ass!" Legend gritted, raising his weapon.

"I didn't torture them…not the kids. That wasn't me, I swear! I beat all them charges after they ran the DNA, but I got held up on some other shit, so I had to do a bid. And I was only tryin' to help mama! I didn't know she would get hooked on that shit. I was using it too! I was using it to forget about all the shit Gene did to me. I just wanted to help," Quentin said in between grimacing in pain.

I saw Legend clench his teeth and something menacing passed through his dark eyes. Quan must have seen it too. He tried to intervene, but it was too late.

"Legend—"

Pow!

Raising his weapon, Legend shot Quentin in the other thigh. The sound of the bullet, though partially silenced, echoed through my brain.

"Aaaarrrrrrgggggghh!" Quentin screamed out finally, as he grabbed at his other leg in agony. My heart clenched in my chest and my stomach lurched. I felt like I was going to throw up as I watched, my eyes fixated on the horrible scene before me.

Both holes in Quentin's legs seeped out his crimson red lifeline as he started to howl in pain, murmuring incoherently while clutching at both of his wounds. Suddenly, Legend dropped his weapon to the ground and took off his shirt, exposing his muscular and heavily tattooed chest. Leaning down, he grabbed Quentin by the collar and then proceeded to punch him over and over again in the face until his nose began to spurt out blood like a faucet.

"Legend!" Quan started his plea as he began to walk over to where Legend was unmercifully beating Quentin's ass, but Dame and Murk stopped him before he could intervene.

"This needs to happen," Murk said to him with finality in his tone. Swallowing hard, Quan clenched his jaw and looked on helplessly as Legend pulverized their brother.

The sound of bone crushing brought tears to my eyes. My stomach began to feel queasy as I heard the sickening sound of blood squishing through with each power-filled punch. When I looked up and saw how utterly shattered Quan appeared as he watched his twin get slaughtered by his youngest brother, I couldn't take it anymore and before I knew it, tears were streaming down my face. Wiping them away, I made a huge mistake and let my eyes fall on where Legend was severely punishing Quentin.

Gritting his teeth tighter with each punch, Legend's fists were completely covered in blood and so was much of his bare chest. But Quentin looked nearly dead. His face was already swollen to shit and his jaw was hanging in a way that I knew meant it was broken. He was lying completely still with his neck twisted in a way that seemed impossible for anyone to manage while still alive. My stomach lurched one more good time and I threw up all over the grass beneath me.

I couldn't take anymore. I couldn't take any of this anymore. It was all way too much.

Chapter Two

LEGEND

After I felt like I was finally satisfied with my work, I stood up and turned to Quan. I knew of all of us, Quan would be the most affected by what I had to do to Quentin. For real, I really wanted to kill his ass, but I knew that if I killed Quentin in front of Quan, I would lose another one of my brothers forever. That's the *only* thing that stopped me. Cush, Murk, Dame, and Quan were all I had left of my family and I needed every one of them.

"Get your brother, Quan. Take him to the hospital," I told him as I grabbed my shirt to wipe off the blood on my body.

Nodding his head, Quan silently walked towards Quentin but I stopped him right before he reached him.

"The only reason I spared him was because of you. I don't give a fuck about that nigga. But if he fucks up again, you know what you gotta do. You bear the weight of his bullshit," I told him. "Just get him out my fuckin' city."

"I know and I will," Quan said quietly. "Let me handle this and I swear if it goes wrong, I won't stand in the way of what comes next. I can't explain it but I just gotta make sure that—"

Quentin let out a loud wheezing noise, stopping Quan from speaking. I nodded my head at him to let him know that he could do what he had to do. He didn't have to explain because I got it. Just like I would do anything when it came to Cush or any of my other brothers, he felt that same connection with Quentin since he was his twin. Unfortunately, any connection I had with Quentin had died a long time ago, and I would never give a fuck about that nigga.

Ever.

"Neesy, you good?" I asked, reaching out to her.

She turned towards me as she wiped at her mouth with her sleeve, but shrunk away from my hand. I looked down and realized that my fingers were still covered in blood and figured that's why she was moving away.

"Come on, let's get into the house," I told her. She didn't say anything, but she stood up on her trembling legs while holding her stomach. I moved to touch her when she looked like she would fall over, but she held her hand out to stop me.

"No! I'm fine," she told me. "Don't touch me."

Shocked, I frowned as I watched her stagger to the house on her own. Something was up with her and I would most definitely be finding out what the fuck it was. After how I'd just handled business, you'd think she would be grateful. I was expecting pussy not pressure. She was acting like I wronged her ass.

"Aye, I'mma head out," Murk told me. "Me and Dame can take

care of Mello's bitch on our own. You handle your business, L."

"A'ight," was all I said with a frown covering my face.

My mind was officially fucked up as I tried to think of possible reasons why Shanecia could be acting the way she was. She didn't want me to touch her. Was it because of what she'd overheard from Quentin about what Gene had almost done to me?

I threw my keys to Murk so that he and Dame could leave, and took off towards the house. At the moment, I couldn't deal with Shanecia. I needed to take a shower and settle my mind first before I went down the road with her about what had happened in my past. Never in my life did I think I would have to speak to her about what went on with Gene when we were little and, from how she was already acting, I really was afraid to.

SHANECIA

I wasn't sure where I was going to go but I had to leave where I was. There was too much going on and, even though it seemed like I was always the last person to be told anything, I was always the one getting pulled into shit. Legend had so much about his past that he felt he needed to hide, but when that same past came back to get him, I was the one who got caught up in his shit.

The fact of the matter was, as much as I loved him, I needed a break from everything so that I could experience some normal shit. *Boring* shit. I wanted my old life back. Everything going on here was too much for me. And besides the drama, Legend was barely home anyways. I spent most of my days pretty much alone because he was out fighting his battles in the street. All of his enemies saw me as his weak link, it seemed, because I couldn't keep my ass from getting kidnapped. I was done with this shit.

Walking towards our room, I had to pass by the room where Cush was sleeping in and I stopped when I heard light sniffles coming from behind the door. I paused for a few seconds to listen before knocking and pushing the door open.

Cush was sitting on the bed with her legs pulled up and her arms wrapped around them. Her chin was resting on top of her knees as she cried. I didn't even have to ask why. Her room had a clear view of the front yard. I already knew what was bothering her.

"Legend... Legend took care of everything. You're safe...there is no reason to cry," I told her.

Sitting down on the bed, I reached out to touch her but then thought twice and stood back up. Walking into her bathroom, I rinsed my mouth out with mouthwash before returning to her side as she continued to cry.

"Spray some of that body spray on yourself too," she added with a light laugh as she continued wiping tears from her eyes.

With a small smile, I did as she asked although I figured she was joking and sat down in the chair across from her.

"You want to talk?" I asked her. "You don't have to. I just wanted to make sure you were going to be okay."

"I—I just thought that by moving away, I could pretend that this shit wasn't me. That none of the things I'd gone through had ever happened. Everyone in New York thinks I'm some trust fund heiress to some rich entertainers from Miami or something. No one knows about my real life or what my brothers do in order to give me what I need. Quentin returning reminded me about how fucked up I am. I can't even date seriously because of him. As much as I try to move on from what he's done to me, I can't forget it. He ruined my life."

Pausing for a minute, she let out a bit of a forced laugh before starting back.

"And even if it weren't for that stopping me from dating…how do you explain to someone you're with that your brothers are trying their hardest to be the kingpins of Miami? Legend moved me away because he said I didn't like to listen. I was happy to move away from this shit. I don't want to come back to it but I guess I have to, right? If Quentin wasn't the one who was in my apartment...that means someone else was there, right? Probably one of Mello's men. Legend will never let me leave!"

But I can leave.

The thought came to my mind before I knew it. Brushing it away, I put my hand on Cush's knee to comfort her. I needed to give her some encouragement, because she was going to need it. Unfortunately, everything she was saying, I already knew to be true.

"Trust your brothers because they will do what's right when it comes to you. You are their only sister and you're stuck with them. They have vowed to protect you, so let them do that. You'll be fine," I told her.

Pursing her lips, a hint of doubt crossed through her eyes but she still shot me a smile and nodded her head. I stood up and gave her a hug before walking out of the room and going into mine. When I stepped inside, I heard the shower running and knew Legend was already bathing away his brother's blood.

Walking over to the nightstand, I grabbed his phone and dialed a number that I knew by heart.

"Hello?"

"Darin...can I stay with you for a few days?" I asked him in a quiet but rushed tone.

"Neesy? Of course you can," he told me. "Is something going on?"

Tears came to my eyes but I bit my bottom lip and pushed them away.

"I'm going back to Spelman, but I need to stay with you until I can verify that my housing permit is still active and that I'm still officially enrolled. I'll explain more when I get there," I told him.

"When will you be here? Do you need a ride?" he asked.

"I'll drive over soon. Not sure when yet. I still have my car, so I can get over there myself," I informed him.

The water to the shower cut off suddenly and I felt the feeling of mild panic building up in my body.

"I have to go. I don't have my cellphone, but I'll try to find it. I'll see you later."

Hanging up the phone, I deleted the call. I brushed the tears away from my eyes and sat down on the bed, trying to make sense of my thoughts.

"What's wrong with you?" Legend asked as he walked in from the adjoining bathroom.

I turned around to look at him. His damp chest was no longer covered with blood and he had a towel wrapped around his waist. As much as I loved him, not even looking at him could ease my mind. My eyes went to his fists that were bruised red from how hard he'd pummeled Quentin's face. A timorous shudder travelled down my spine and I looked away.

"Nothing," I lied as I lay down on the bed, turning my face towards the wall so I didn't have to see him. "I'm just tired."

There was a long silence and I felt like my throat was closing up, cutting off my ability to breathe. Although I wasn't looking at him, I could feel Legend's hard stare on me.

He knows I'm lying, I thought to myself. He knows something isn't right.

And it wasn't. Deep down I knew that it wouldn't ever be right because as much as I loved him, I wasn't mentally prepared for what it took to be his woman. I couldn't live like this any longer.

"This…this isn't because of what Quentin said, is it? About what his dad did to him…that he tried to do to—"

"Oh God no," I said quickly, shaking my head. I turned to look him right in his eyes.

"What he tried to do to you was sick…you were a child. I wish you would have talked to me about it, but I can see why you didn't. *This* has nothing to do with that," I assured him with certainty.

"Well, what does *this* have to do with?" he asked me, still looking uneasy about what I said and a little doubtful that what I'd said was true.

"Nothing. I told you, I'm fine. Just tired," I repeated and laid back down on the bed.

"Okay," he said finally, his voice suddenly light and airy as if we weren't having the most distant and awkward moment of our relationship. "I gotta go to the warehouse to take care of some business and I'll be back."

"Okay," I replied softly as a tear fell down my cheek.

Biting my lip, I listened as he moved around the room getting dressed and ready to leave. By the time he returned, I would be gone.

Chapter Three

MALIAH

I *really can't believe this shit!* I thought to myself as I clanged pots in the kitchen.

I had told everybody that I was in the kitchen cooking, but I couldn't do shit. My mind was gone as the image of Danny and Alicia kept creeping its way back in. How the *hell* did that shit happen? There were plenty of things that I could have created in my mind of what Danny's crack head ass could do while he was high, but sleeping with Alicia was definitely not one of them!

"I see your legs working," Murk's deep voice echoed from behind me. "But why you droppin' pots and shit? Daddy's dick still got you fucked up in the head?"

Turning around, my eyes fell on Murk's sexy ass smile and my mood changed instantly. A fluttery feeling surged through my stomach as I thought back to hours ago when he was beating it up in the garage. Licking my lips, I wondered if I could get another dose, but then the image of Danny and Alicia crossed through my mind and my mood instantly changed.

"I just have a lot on my mind," I told him, averting my gaze as I hoped he wouldn't ask any further about what I was talking about.

Nodding his head, he reached over and grabbed an apple from the countertop and took a large bite out of it. My eyes went to his hands which had a fresh cut on it. It was a surface cut, not enough to draw a large amount of blood, but it still made me wonder about what he'd been up to and also about something that had been on my mind for days.

"Did you try to kill Danny?" I found myself asking all of a sudden. "Just tell me the truth…please. I need to know."

Although Danny was about as dead to me as his dick was the night we almost had sex, I still needed to know. I knew that my mind wouldn't be able to rest unless I knew for sure if Murk had tried to kill someone who had, until recently, meant so much to me and who still meant the world to my kids.

Lifting his head, Murk chewed slowly on the apple and looked me directly in my eyes. His face was expressionless but his eyes were full of many emotions. I could tell that he was wondering if he should tell me the truth. I could see that he was hesitant, probably because he was unsure of what my reaction would be.

"Tell me," I pushed eagerly, pleading to him with my eyes.

"Yes."

He said it so quickly that if I hadn't been looking right at him when he said it, I would have missed it. Tears clouded my vision and I wasn't prepared for that reaction. But it wasn't because of Danny.

For some reason, although I knew that Murk wasn't a law abiding citizen, him admitting that he'd really tried to kill Danny almost made my heart stop and a peculiar feeling came over me. I felt afraid; similar to the feeling I'd felt the first time that he'd seen me when I'd approached him with Shanecia at the rec center. Yes, I loved him but the fear was still there.

"Why?" I croaked out in a small voice.

Dropping my head, I darted my eyes to the side and blinked back the tears that they'd been cradling. I felt Murk move in front of me and then the next thing I knew, his hand was on my chin, lifting my head up so that my eyes met his.

"I couldn't just stand by and let a nigga put his hands on the woman I loved. I didn't know it then but I loved you and that's why I had to do it. I knew it wasn't my situation, but I couldn't keep myself from doing what I had to do."

Pausing, Murk bit his lip and looked away for a moment. When his eyes fell back on me, he was staring at me in a way so true and so sincere, it almost caused me discomfort…as if I were seeing him in a way I wasn't supposed to.

"There is no way I will ever be able to stop myself from destroying someone who has hurt you…or the kids. I know you might want me to be a different man but I can't. And I won't even try."

Without speaking, we stared into each other's eyes, speaking to one another without words. In the intensity of his stare, I felt as if I were understanding things about him that I never had before, as he also began to understand more about me.

Suddenly, he grabbed me in his arms and placed his lips on mine, sucking my bottom lip between his. Running his hand behind my back, he locked his massive hand over one of my ass cheeks and squeezed hard. By the time he broke our kiss, my panties were soaking wet.

"So what we cooking?" he asked me, licking his lips.

Unable to readily respond but happy for the subject change, I continued to stare at him with eyelids heavy from the lust that I felt.

"Huh?" I asked, shaking myself fully awake when I saw him walk over and peek at the ingredients I'd pulled out and placed on the counter. "What do you mean 'we'?"

"I mean, I'mma help you in here. We gone do this shit together," he replied with a smirk. "You always watchin' them reruns of them black married people cookin' together so let's get it."

Laughing, I shook my head. "This coming from the same man who said 'making love' was some 'gay shit' you wasn't cool with? You sure you wanna be in here cooking with me?"

His face frowned up in disgust but he nodded his head 'yes'. It was almost like his body was battling itself just to do a simple nod. I laughed again as I watched the look on his face. He was trying to change to become the man he thought a woman like me wanted, but what he didn't understand was all I wanted was him. There was no change necessary to be the one for me. I loved Murk just as he was.

"Baby, go shower up or somethin'. You don't need to worry about what we're eating. I got you," I told him with a wink.

Murk's face relaxed instantly and he shot me a smile as he walked by. Slapping me on my ass, he left me giggling as he walked out of the kitchen and down the hall. What we had was far from perfect. Actually, it wasn't even close. But at the same time, I knew I couldn't and wouldn't trade Murk for anyone else in the world.

*****

"Li, wake up…Li…damn! Nigga, wake up!"

I felt Murk nudging me and I also heard every word he was saying, but I was dead tired and couldn't move. I couldn't even remember falling asleep but after cooking and getting the kids to bed, I fell out and went into a coma-like sleep that I didn't want to get up from, but Murk was trying his hardest to wake me up. He was working my last nerve.

"What, Pablo?!" I fussed as I reached out and swatted his hand away from the breast he was squeezing.

"Man, wake up and stop with that 'Pablo' shit. My dick hard!" he grumbled, emphasizing the latter part of his statement as if that was the selling point.

Normally whenever Murk wanted it, I was ready to give it to him. But he'd already worn my ass out earlier so I was physically spent and, after seeing Danny and Alicia, I was emotionally spent too. Not to mention disgusted.

"Murk, I'm tired!" I argued, snatching the covers up under my chin.

"Nigga, you ain't tired!"

My eyes flew open when he grabbed the covers and pulled them straight off of me, exposing my body to the icy chill in the room. He was so gotdamn annoying sometimes!

"Why you playin', Murk?!" I yelled as I sat up in the bed and reached for the covers. He batted them out of the way. Grumbling under my breath, I reached down again to grab them and that's when my eyes finally fell on what he had in his hand.

"Oh my God!" I shrieked as I grabbed at the tiny black box. "Is that a—"

My face fell when I opened up the small ring box and there wasn't a damn thing inside. Frowning, I crooked my head up and looked at Murk sideways. What kind of game was this nigga playing, waking me up to give me an empty ass box?

"What the hell is this?" I asked him, dangling the box in front of his face as I held it between two fingers.

Smirking, he licked his lips over his gold teeth before he began to speak.

"It's a promise box," he told me as if that was supposed to explain everything.

I gawked at him as if he'd lost his damn mind. Probably because he had!

"Murk, what the hell is a 'promise box'? I've heard of a promise ring…hell, you could have even given me a damn promise bracelet or necklace. Who gives somebody an empty ass box?!"

Reaching out, he playfully nudged me against my jaw as he laughed. It only served to deepen my frown. I didn't see a damn thing funny. I tossed the box at his head and he caught it just in time before it clipped him right across his smiling face.

Crossing my arms in front of my chest, I laid back on the bed and waited for him to explain with my eyes narrowed into slits.

"A promise box means that, at some point, I'm planning on marrying ya mean ass," Murk started, still holding that sexy ass smirk on his face. "I want you to keep this on the dresser. And when I think the time is right, I promise to put a big ass, colossal ass diamond in this muthafucka."

His explanation done, he stared at me, still grinning, as if I was supposed to jump in his arms or something. What the hell did I care about a damn box and a promise for? He hadn't broken any actual bread, so he really didn't make a sacrifice in making this so-called promise to me.

"Murk, the whole point of buying a promise ring is so that when I walk around, it's on my finger as a constant reminder to me and everyone around me that I'm taken!" I said with frustration, waving my hands in the air. "And it's supposed to cost you something! Niggas drop stacks on rings because it shows you serious! But nooooo, you wanna give me an empty ass box and promise that you gone put something in it sometime before we die!"

Rolling my eyes, I laid back down and rolled over, turning my back to him.

This nigga got me fucked up, I thought to myself.

He might as well just did what all the other niggas in the hood did and don't say shit about marriage. Just let a bitch pretend in her mind that one day it would finally happen.

"I had a feelin' your mean ass would say something like that," he said with a chuckle from behind me.

I rolled my eyes and once they refocused, I saw that he'd moved and placed his hand right in front of my face. I was about to swat him away until he extended his two fingers, which were holding a nice sized solitaire diamond ring. I gasped as soon as I saw it. It was absolutely beautiful.

"So, see? I did break some bread for your ungrateful ass," he muttered from behind me. "How else would I have gotten that damn empty ass box?"

"Oh my God! It's so pretty—"

I moved to grab it from his hand but Murk snatched the ring away before I could. Frowning, I sat up and looked at him, watching as he pulled his chain off from around his neck and placed the ring on it.

"What are you doin'?!"

"I'm wearing it because I don't think your ass deserves it yet," he replied back. "The next time a nigga gives you an empty box, you better be happy about that shit."

And with that, he laid down on his back and closed his eyes as the beautiful ring glistened from its place right in the middle of his chest.

He had me *all the way* fucked up.

Reaching out, I snatched the chain and unlatched it so fast he barely had time to react. By the time he sat up, I'd already begun to place the ring on my finger, right where it belonged.

"Maliah! What da fuck, man?" Murk yelled as he grabbed the chain from my hand. "You nearly burnt the skin off my neck from how hard you pulled at this damn chain!"

He was fuming, but I was happy as hell as I stared at the rock on my finger. Wiggling my fingers back and forth, I watched the sparkle as it glistened in the dim lighting in the room.

"You like it?" he asked with a smile and I nodded my head and then leaned over to give him a kiss on the lips.

It was beautiful.

Chapter Four

SHANECIA

"Okay, now that you're all settled in, can you tell me why you're here?" Darin asked as he sat down next to me.

Sighing, my eyes fell on Tanecia's wide and expectant eyes. She was lying, slightly raised up, on the bed with her arms crossed, waiting for me to explain as well. Her mouth was pressed in a thin line but her expression was otherwise unreadable.

"I'm leaving him," I admitted quietly. A short stint of silence followed and I tittered a bit, already struggling with myself to stay firm in my decision.

"Who?" Darin asked with his brows tightly knitted together across his wrinkled forehead.

"Legend."

"WHAT?!" the both of them yelled out so loudly it stung my ears.

Exchanging matching looks of bewilderment, they each looked at each other briefly as if having a silent conversation through their eyes before turning back to me.

I couldn't blame them. I could barely believe it myself. Legend and I had built up a love like none other I'd ever experienced in the matter of a few months. Not only had I never thought that I would want to leave him, especially not so soon, but neither did anyone else.

But like the old folks say, what starts fast ends even faster. Relationships that came from instant passion was quick to light and fast to burn, until there was nothing left. The flame I had in my heart for Legend was still there, far more powerful than just a mild simmer. But, at the moment, it wasn't enough to make me stay. I had to leave.

"Neesy…I'm not a fan of him or his brothers, but I have to admit I didn't see this shit coming," Darin replied. "He didn't hurt you, did he?"

A tear escaped my eyes and fell down my cheek. Reaching up, I quickly brushed it away and shook my head.

"No, he would never hurt me and I know that. But I—I just can't live this lifestyle with him. My whole reason for going to school is to get a better life for myself. I never wanted to be caught up in a life of crime and that's exactly where he's put me," I told them honestly.

When I looked up, Tanecia's eyes were focused on some space behind me and I had a feeling she was deep in her own personal thoughts about her life. Then her eyes shot over to Darin and I saw her cheeks tinge red.

What the hell is she thinking? I thought to myself. I was just about to ask when Darin cut in.

"Well, you can't stay here," he said point-blank.

Frowning and confused, I brushed another tear away and looked

34

at him.

"What do you mean?" I looked from him to Tanecia who was now frowning as well. Darin held his hand up to stop her from speaking when she opened her mouth.

"I don't mean that you can't stay here because I don't want you to. I mean that as soon as Legend finds out you've left him, he's coming here and I'm not sure you're prepared to deal with that right now, because you know he will have zero understanding about the whole thing. So if you really want to leave, you gotta leave ASAP. You need to go back to Spelman now…get a hotel or something until your apartment is ready. I'll help you," he offered.

"He's right," Tanecia chimed in. "Let me tell you, niggas don't give up easily. Even after Mello beat my ass for getting pregnant, he still tried to get back with me for a minute. I guess until wifey found out."

An awkward silence hung between us as everyone kept their thoughts about Tanecia's comment in their head. I didn't like her comparison of Mello to Legend, but I decided to keep my mouth shut. Although they were different, many parts of them were very alike and those were the parts that I wasn't comfortable with.

"Is Legend usually gone all night?" Darin asked me.

Somewhat ashamed to admit it, I nodded my head. Although I knew that Legend wasn't out all night dealing with other women, it still made me feel some kind of way to admit that he was always gone.

"Stay the night and I'll get you a flight that leaves out in the morning," Darin continued. "At least get some rest. I'll get the other room set up for you."

I nodded quietly and tried my best to give him a thin smile as he stood up to leave. Once he closed the door behind him, I turned to Tanecia.

"What's on your mind?" I asked her. "And don't lie because it's all over your face that you're thinking about something."

Tanecia shook her head slightly, allowing the cornrows I'd braided for her to drape over one shoulder.

"You were talking and what you were saying just reminded me of how fuckin' stupid I am in comparison to you. I'm supposed to be the older sister, but you're always the one making the wise decisions." She tried to smile with her lips but it didn't reach her eyes which were still pointed downwards at the ends.

"Well, you're lucky you have Darin," I told her as I reached out to smooth down a few fuzzy pieces of her hair that were sticking straight up in the air.

Tanecia snorted out a laugh and wiped a lone tear from her cheek that had escaped her eye.

"You've always had Darin," I continued, more depth to my meaning than she may have understood. "You should let him be there for you, Tan. In more ways than you have thus far. Can't you see that he wants to be?"

I watched her nod her head but in my mind, I couldn't stop myself from thinking about Legend, and if I was sure of what I was doing. What we had was natural. It was the best kind of love; the kind that blossomed in a way that wasn't forced. We fell for each other freely, with no expectations of anything other than that we'd stay true to one another and be happy.

And that's what he'd given me but at the moment, I was scared. When his street life leaked over to our personal life, the image I had of us was shattered and I saw through to the part of him that created those whispers in the hood about his ruthless nature. He would never stop having enemies, because he would never relinquish his control of Miami and that meant that I'd always be his weak spot. His chick…the easy target.

My leaving wasn't totally selfish; it was also to save him. I was from the hood but I wasn't hood…not in the way it counted anyways. As much as Legend tried to teach me the rules of the game, I was still naïve. If anything happened to me and it was because of Legend's lifestyle, it would destroy him. I knew it because he'd told me countless times. So as much as I told everybody that me leaving was for me. It really wasn't only for me. I was trying to protect him too.

"You sure you'll be able to get over him?" Tanecia asked me, pulling my focus back to her eyes.

I hadn't even known until that moment that she was watching me so intently, as if she could literally read my thoughts as they formed in my head. Returning her gaze, I bit my lip and shook my head 'no' because it was the truth that I felt in my soul.

No matter how hard I tried, I would never get over Legend.

Chapter Five

LEGEND

"Is this the one you want?" the brown-skinned girl in front of me asked as she smiled, showing off damn near every one of her pearly white teeth.

"Yeah," I said in a low tone and watched as she reached down and grabbed the chocolate cupcake I'd pointed at.

Her eyes flicked up to my face as she bent down low, showing off the top of her bouncy, round B-cup tits. She was sexy, I had to give her that. And if I were any other man who didn't give a fuck about my chick, I would have definitely hit but I wasn't any other man.

Plus, this kind of shit happened to me all the time. I knew damn well I wasn't no ugly nigga and then, on top of that, it was like women could smell the money on me. They always flirted and I always resisted. Even if I wasn't with Shanecia, no chick working at a bakery could pull me.

"I didn't take you for a cupcake man," she teased with a smile as she placed it in a box for me.

Raising my eyes, I gave her a hard look. I thought about not replying back but then decided to go ahead and put her on notice.

"I'm not. It's for my girl. She likes when a nigga does all this sweet shit," I replied, watching the smile melt away from her face.

As I continued to stare at her, I couldn't help admiring her for cutting off all the charm as soon as I mentioned I had a girl. Usually hearing that a nigga had a chick didn't matter to other women who came on to me. They didn't give a fuck who I had if they thought they could convince me to let her take Shanecia's place or at least come in at a close second. But the mere mention of Shanecia instantly put her in full business mode and she cut off all that smiling and teasing shit with the quickness.

"That'll be $3.49," she informed curtly.

"Damn! $3.50 for a fuckin' cupcake?" I joked as I shot her a five-dollar bill over the counter.

"$3.50 for the *best* kind of fuckin' cupcakes," she corrected me with a wink as she handed me my change. I took it and tossed it in the tip jar.

"I hope your girl enjoys them. I made them myself this morning and it's a new recipe I'm trying out."

For some reason her comment made me look at her name tag.

Belisa, I read in my mind.

Then something dawned on me. The name of the small cupcake shop was Belisa's Cupcakes. She was the owner. I felt her eyes on me and when I glanced at her, I could tell she knew I'd discovered that she was more than some broad who worked at a bakery. She owned the place.

"I'm sure she'll enjoy them," I replied with a nod.

Grabbing the cupcake, I turned around and walked out. She said something, but I didn't respond. I was a lot of things but I wasn't stupid by a long shot. I'd already admired her too many damn times in the five minutes I'd been standing there. It was time for me to go home to Shanecia.

Ten minutes later, I walked into the house with the cupcake in my hand, prepared to surprise Shanecia with it so I could talk to her about whatever was on her mind.

Something wasn't right with her and I could sense that shit as easily as if her feelings were my own, and I was hoping like hell she wasn't feeling some kind of way about what Quentin had said. So instead of dealing with the questioning of Mello's wife myself, I passed the duties off to Dame and Murk before calling it an early night. I figured that coming home early with one of her favorite snacks would make up for the events of earlier, but when I came home and she was nowhere to be found, I knew I was dead wrong.

"Cush!" I yelled as I dropped the cupcake down on the table in my bedroom and stormed down the hall to her door.

When I pushed it open, she was sitting on the bed with a guilt-ridden look on her face. She already knew what was up.

"Where the hell is she?!" I barked, standing in front of my sister with my arms folded across my chest.

"She left," Cush replied in a quiet tone. "She said she was going back to Spelman."

My anger seethed to an ultimate high. I felt like my blood was boiling. How could she make a fuckin' decision like that and not even think to talk to me? How could she decide to leave me without even giving a nigga an explanation? Who does that bullshit?

"Why the fuck didn't you call me to tell me she was leaving?" I yelled at Cush, making tears come to her eyes.

"Because I sympathize with her, Leith! I'm jealous of her. If I could leave all this shit behind and live a different life, I would too!" she burst out as if she had been waiting for years to finally get that information off her chest.

"How could you say that shit, Cush? I'm your fuckin' brother and all I've done is look out for you. I've taken care of you your whole life to make sure that you had everything you could ever want. What da fuck you mean you wish you could live a different life? You don't want me as your brother?" I asked with my eyes narrowed.

Lowering her eyes and cutting them to the side, she hesitated for a second too long for my taste.

"Really, Cush?!" I asked her feeling a pang of some emotion I hadn't felt a long time in my chest. "Really? So what you really want is to be on your own and live your own life, huh?"

Wiping the tears from her eyes, she turned sharply, looking at me so deeply and with so much pain in her eyes that it made my throat feel tight. Whatever she was about to say, I knew I wouldn't like it, but I knew it was going to be the God honest truth.

"I love you, Leith, but this life y'all chose is what you chose. I don't want anything to do with it. I don't want the enemies that you've created coming after me just because they found out I'm your sister. I don't want to think about muthafuckas climbing through my damn window! Women don't want to deal with that shit every day. We just want to live, be loved, and be happy. You don't get that and Neesy and I both know that. You'll never change and that's why she left," she told me easily as if she didn't know how much her words stung me as they came out.

"Well, you can leave too," I told her coolly as I wiped the sweat off my forehead with my forearm. It wasn't even hot in the house, but I was so fuckin' mad that I was burning the hell up.

"I'll keep depositing money in your account to make sure that you're taken care of but if to be rid of me is what you want, then so be it. Don't visit and don't call me no more."

"Leith—"

Placing my hand in the air, I stopped her from speaking. I knew she thought I was being an asshole, but I just couldn't deal with all this shit right now. Shanecia was gone and now Cush was tripping right along with her, even though we both knew Cush's crazy ass wasn't going nowhere. It seemed like every time I made some progress on Mello, my personal life took the biggest muthafuckin' nosedive into some bullshit.

"Pack your stuff up and I'll get you a flight back home for tonight. Call one of your other brothers so they can take your ass to the airport," I told her as I walked out of her room.

Behind me, I heard her suck her teeth.

"Legend, you're takin' this shit too serious. Let me explain!"

Shaking my head, I continued walking. There wasn't any explanation necessary. I'd let Cush have her way for now and she could leave. I'd just have to deal with her ass later. I learned a long time ago that if a muthafucka wanted to go, you needed to let that muthafucka go.

All except for Shanecia. She wasn't taking her big head ass anywhere and the quicker I got her to realize that shit, the better.

*****

Boom! Boom! Boom!

"Open up this muthafuckin' door!" I yelled as I continued to beat the door with my fist.

Trying my hardest to knock the shit straight off the hinges, I continued to knock against it, making it rattle more and more with each hit.

About two seconds later, I heard the locks shifting and I backed away, crossing my arms at my chest. When it swung open, the first person I saw was Darin. He was fully dressed and didn't look surprised at all to see me.

"So your dumb ass already know why the fuck I'm here, huh?" I questioned as I pushed by him and walked right into his house. "Neesy, get the fuck out here and eat this muthafuckin' cupcake so you can come to your fuckin' senses!"

I slammed the cupcake box down on the table and walked down the hall towards the room that Shanecia had stayed in the few nights she would stay over to be with her sister. When I entered in the room, I was shocked to see that it was empty and the bed was made. None of her clothes were inside. She wasn't there.

"Where the fuck is she?" I asked Darin when I heard him walk up behind me.

The nonchalant look on his face was pissing me off more and more by the second. I didn't have any issues with his lame ass, but he was about to change all of that if he didn't open his damn mouth and tell me where Shanecia was.

"She's not here," he replied with ease.

"Well no shit, Detective McDumbass," I grit through my teeth. "If she was here, do you think I would be askin' your stupid ass where *the fuck* she is?!"

From the way Darin bit down hard on the back of his teeth, I could tell he didn't appreciate how I was talking to him in his own house, but I didn't give a single fuck. If he wasn't wasting my time by stating the obvious, I would have already left out his shit and been on my way.

"She's already on a plane headed back to Spelman. She's going to see if she can get her spot back."

Raising my hand to my head, I pressed down hard on my temples before running my hand down over my face.

"Why the *hell* would she do that?! Why would she leave without telling me?"

Darin started to open his mouth and I shook my head at him

before he could even get a word out.

"No offense, nigga, but I don't want to hear shit you gotta say. For real, I should fuck you up for being in on this shit and not lettin' me know but I won't because yo' chick in there," I told him, pointing down the hall to where I knew Tanecia was.

"Legend, stop!" a voice suddenly called out, nearly stopping my heart.

Once I overcame my shock, I glared at Darin. If he was any other nigga, he would have been tongue kissing the fuck out of the barrel of my gun.

"Muthafucka, I thought you said she was already gone, witcho lyin' ass!" I spat as I started to walk in the direction of her voice. "I owe you an ass whoopin' when I'm done talking. Don't think about going nowhere, nigga! And if I forget you better remind me too!" I called out over my shoulder.

Darin made a scoffing sound as I walked away but I was dead ass serious. That was some fuckin' bitch shit he was on. I can understand that he was Shanecia's friend and all, but he was a man and men didn't do that shit. Shit, he could have winked or something to let me know what was up.

As soon as I walked into the room where Tanecia had been the last time I was there, the first person my eyes fell on was Shanecia, sitting in the chair next to her sister with a suitcase at her feet. Just seeing it made my blood boil to the point that I had to close my eyes to calm myself down. She'd actually had time to think about the shit she was planning on doing and went through with it anyways. How could she just up and leave me?

"What the hell you doin', Neesy?! You was just gonna leave without tellin' yo' nigga shit? As much as your ass keeps gettin' kidnapped and shit, and you thought this was a smart idea?" I yelled with narrowed eyes as I stood over her.

Her eyes were red and puffy. She'd been crying and, even now, she still was cradling her tears in her eyes as she bit her lip and tried to keep them from falling. Still, I wasn't moved at all by her dramatics.

"You need to hurry up and say some shit that will convince me that you ain't lost your muthafuckin' mind, Neesy!"

"I just want to leave, Legend!" she cried out as the tears let loose and began falling down her cheeks. "We've only been together over the summer and I've had to deal with people taking me, almost being killed, being drugged...I just want my old life back!"

Seeing her so upset, made me try to calm down although her words were bringing me to a panic. She couldn't really want to leave, could she? The love we had wasn't built over a long amount of time and, yes, we only had a summertime romance. But that wasn't all I wanted it to be. I loved Shanecia more than I'd ever loved anyone. Call it infatuation, obsession...call it whatever the fuck you wanted to. I just wanted her to the point that it wasn't a want any longer. I needed her with me. Everyone was leaving me right now. I *needed* her to stay.

"Shanecia," I started, using her whole name. "With me is where you need to be. I can protect you, ma. I'm sorry you feeling some type of way but that's too bad...you gotta stay."

Biting down on my back teeth, I thought about dropping down

to my knees and begging her. That's how tore up she had me feeling right then. Legend never bowed down to anyone for any reason. That was something I lived by. But in that moment, I actually wondered if I should do it for Shanecia and whether it would keep her from leaving me.

But before I could even think on it further, she opened up her mouth and said the most fucked up shit of all.

"But you *can't* protect me, Legend! Ever since I've been with you, all you've done is place me in danger. Before you, I didn't have to deal with this shit! I didn't worry about who was going to come hurt me just for walking to the store, or if I'm safe on campus when I go to school. Fuckin' with you is going to kill me. I don't want to be with you anymore…I don't want any of this!"

Wow, was the single word that came to my mind.

And just like that, I realized that even the strongest love couldn't stand against my pride. Hearing Shanecia declare that I couldn't protect her, that I'd *failed* at being a man for her, changed something in me. If she wanted to leave, I was done standing in her way.

With a curt nod, I pressed my lips together and turned around swiftly, making my all-white Jordans squeak as I strode to the door. She didn't call out for me to stop the way Cush had but it didn't surprise me. Cush had been speaking through temporary feelings, the way that I had spoken to her. She was my blood and she could never leave me no matter how much I upset her. But Shanecia meant every word that she said and I was willing to let her have her way.

If she didn't want to fuck with a nigga, she no longer had to. I was through.

Chapter Six

MALIAH

Two Weeks Later

"FUCK!" I cursed as I winded my hips into Murk's face.

His thick, juicy lips were wrapped around my clit as he held it securely between them and ran his tongue back and forth over my nub. The shit he did made me feel like I could take a flight on Cloud 9. He was the absolute best at what he did to me between the sheets and I was convinced that there was none better. Matter of fact, if anybody tried to *tell* me that there was one better, I'd beat that bitch's ass for telling me a gotdamn lie.

"Hold still," he mumbled as he placed his hands on each side of my big ass.

I didn't pay him the least bit of attention. He'd worked his magic and was bringing me right to the brink of an orgasm. There was no stopping it now.

"Hold *still*," he repeated, gripping my ass harder. But him holding me even tighter only heightened my sexual excitement and I felt my

49

legs began to quiver.

"Shit!" Murk said and released my clit from his mouth.

Flipping me over, he pushed my thick thighs open and pushed his fat, long, and hard rod right in between my juicy folds. Wasting no time at all, he started thrashing hard inside me, immediately making me happy as hell that I hadn't cum already seconds before.

With each thrust, he was pushing me closer and closer to what was about to the biggest orgasm ever. I curled my toes as I felt it began to creep up on me. And just when I thought I couldn't take enough, he reached down and stuck a thumb in my ass with one hand and pinched down hard on my nipple with the other hand. That was all I needed.

"SHIT, MURK!" I yelled as I creamed all over him, immediately feeling my knees go weak.

"We ain't done yet," he told me.

With both hands, he lifted my ass up off the bed and placed my legs over his shoulder. The feel of his curved dick against my G-spot brought me to an immediate state of passion and I was instantly ready to go once again.

By the time we were finished, I'd cum four times and Murk, twice. He hadn't even pulled out this time, which kind of surprised me but I was so lost in the moment, I didn't even care.

"I gotta get in the shower so I can go. I'll be back later on," Murk told me as he jumped out of the bed.

Rolling my eyes, I couldn't help but groan. "When are you goin' to take me somewhere? I'm so sick of being in this damn house."

"What you mean?" Murk asked with a frown right before he walked into the bathroom.

Turning to me, he crossed his arms in front of his chest, his flaccid pole still glistening with my juices as it lay against his thigh.

"I mean, I don't work because you don't want me to and I don't go anywhere because you're always working and we never do anything. We never got to really date..." I said, more to myself than to him as I just realized it was true. "We just got together and immediately started fucking. Is it because I was a stripper? Is that why you never took me on a date?"

"Li, we *did* go on a date! Remember we went with your cousin to—"

Jumping off the bed with the covers wrapped around me, I squinted my eyes at him.

"That wasn't a date! They were going on a trip and you asked me to go because you didn't have anything else to do! And then when we got there, all we did was have sex the whole time! We didn't even get to see anything!"

Murk moved forward, with his hands on his muscular waist, making his back arch in a way that allowed his pole to seemingly point accusingly at me. His hazel eyes bore into me under the hoods of his crumpled eyebrows.

"From what I remember your ass wasn't too concerned with seeing shit! After I laid this dick down, all you wanted to do was go to sleep!" he barked back through his teeth.

Dropping back down onto the bed with defeat, I began to sulk.

Murk just didn't get it and it was starting to get on my nerves. He always thought that all a woman needed in order to be satisfied was some good dick and her bills paid. I needed more than that. Was it wrong that I wanted more from him? Maybe it was.

I heard the shower turn on in the bathroom and five seconds later, Murk closed the door, signaling the end of our conversation. Times like these made me understand why Shanecia left Legend alone. Neither one of them seemed to know what it meant to actually be in a real relationship, and I was starting to think that I may be the first real girlfriend that Murk has ever had.

Rolling over in the bed, I grabbed my cell phone and called Shanecia, praying that she would pick up. The past couple weeks since she returned to Spelman, she'd been diving into her work in order to forget about Legend and it meant that every time I tried to call her, she was either in class and couldn't answer because she was busy or she had to call me right back.

I still hadn't told her about her mother and Danny. At the moment, I didn't think I really needed to. Shanecia didn't even ask about her mother anymore. It seemed like she was trying to leave Miami, and everything in it, behind her. The more she claimed to be busy whenever I called, the more I wondered if she was trying to leave me behind too.

"Hello?"

"Hey stranger," I started, flipping over on my stomach as I held my head up with my hand. "Can you talk or are you busy?"

"Li-Li, don't do that. You know I'm just—"

"Yes, I know," I interrupted her. "You're trying to stay focused so you can keep your mind off Legend. But what does that have to do with me? You know I'm still your cousin, right?"

She replied back with a sigh. "I know and I'm sorry. How are my nieces and nephews doing?"

I rolled my eyes dramatically before I answered.

"They are doing better than ever with my mama and Murk both around to spoil them. I swear that nigga can deal with kids but has no idea how to be with a fuckin' female."

"Trust, I know what you mean," she muttered in a way that let me know she was reflecting on her issues with Legend.

"Do you feel like you made the right choice?" I asked her, hoping that she was okay with me pushing her to think about Legend. But, at the moment, I needed a bit of advice on my situation with Murk, so I hoped she was okay with me pressing her for some information.

"Honestly, I do. Not everything that feels good to you is good for you. I think that's how it is with Legend. In only a few months, he had me to the point that I loved him more than I'd ever loved anyone. Imagine if I would have stayed longer...it would have been impossible for me to leave although I know that living that life with him wasn't for me," she admitted, but the words didn't seem natural. They were forced and came out quickly, as if she'd been telling herself that a dozen times a day but still didn't believe it.

I could hear the sadness in her voice. If leaving Legend was what was best for her, it seemed clear to me that she didn't quite think it was true just yet. Her words were wise but the way she said them let on to her true feelings. She missed him and, as much as she tried to be the only woman on Earth who made all smart decisions when it came to love, I could see that she was in love with that man and would go back to him if he even bothered to simply ask. But from what I heard about Legend, I knew he was just as stubborn as she was. These two were just retarded.

"He still hasn't called you, huh?" I asked, totally forgetting my situation with Murk.

Fact of the matter was I was tired of Murk's ass, but I wasn't *done* with his ass. I could entertain the idea all day but I knew I wasn't going anywhere.

"No, he hasn't. And he probably won't, but that's okay. It's better this way." Her voice cracked and I began to feel guilty for bringing Legend up.

"Okay, Neesy…well, let's talk about something else. You know my birthday is coming up in a week and I know I said I wasn't going to do anything, but now I want to have a party or something," I said as I looked down at my ring.

It was so beautiful and I was about to come up with any reason in the world to invite all the girls from the club around just so I could flash it around in their face.

"Will you come in town for that at least?"

She didn't immediately answer and I knew her mind was still on Legend.

"He's not going to be invited," I told her quickly. "I'm with Murk, but me and Legend ain't really all that cool so he shouldn't want to come anyways. You can just come in for the party and leave right out, okay? Hell, you the only real friend I got so you have to come. I'm just inviting them other bitches at the club so I can show off."

"I'll think about it," was all she said but I took that as a 'yes'. Shanecia couldn't be selfish to save her life. I knew she would be there.

"Alright, I'll call you about that later," I said just as I heard the shower go off. "I love you, chick."

"I love you too, Li-Li," she replied back and then the line went dead.

She sounded terrible as hell and I wanted no parts of that kind of pain. That settled it, I would definitely be keeping Murk's ass and would just figure out a way to train him into what I needed him to be in the process.

"Aye," Murk said as soon as he stepped out of the bathroom. He still had the towel wrapped around his waist and his chest was dripping wet. His eyebrows were pulled together in a tight frown as if he'd been thinking hard about something.

"Yes?"

"When the last time your period came on?" he asked me, catching me completely off guard.

"Um," I thought as I rolled my eyes to my forehead and thought about his question. "About three and a half weeks ago almost. It went off like a week before we made up and you bought me my ring."

"Okay," he replied, nodding his head.

Reaching on the dresser, he grabbed his phone and started jotting something down in his phone.

"So like around the 7th?" he specified.

Crinkling my eyebrows, I nodded my head. "Yeah, that sounds about right. What you doin'?"

"What you mean?" he asked as he continued mashing keys on his phone. "I'm puttin' that shit in my calendar so I don't forget! Your ass is fertile as hell so if I'mma be skeeting up in your ass, I need to make sure I ain't gone get caught up."

"Caught up?" I asked, still frowning. I could feel my face begin to heat up, because I just knew he wasn't trying to say what I thought.

"Caught up…as in gettin' your baby makin' ass pregnant. I ain't got time for that shit! We got enough jits walkin' around this bitch," he mumbled absentmindedly as he continued pecking into his phone.

Biting my lip, I stopped myself from cursing his rude ass out. What the hell I wanted to trap his ass up for? He wasn't acting like a prize!

Licking his lips, Murk set his phone down on the dresser and focused his hazel eyes in on mine, softening his stare the more he stared deeply at me. A smirk rose up on his face, starting from the right side before spreading to the left. I relaxed instantly and fell deeper in love. Yes, it was just that easy. His intense gaze could soothe the most heated fires within me and, in seconds, I'd be making all kinds of excuses for his behavior and giving myself reasons as to why I shouldn't take him so seriously.

"I'll be back in a few hours. I'll call you when I'm on my way back. Be dressed and ready to go," he told me, doing that sexy ass thing with his tongue that captivated me the first time I met him.

Without waiting for a response, he walked back into the bathroom and shut the door behind him.

That's the kind of shit that makes me so confused, I thought to myself as I shook my head and fell back on the bed. My stomach was fluttering and my lady lips below were begging for more of his attention.

That's why I can never let go.

Murk could go from shit to sugar in a matter of minutes. I swear I didn't know what to do with his bipolar ass.

Chapter Seven

LEGEND

"On God, I don't understand muthafuckin' females, man," Quan fumed as we all sat in the warehouse.

It had become more like a meeting place for niggas in the recent days. More than anything, we were meeting up at the spot to talk shit about women, drink Heinekens, smoke, and chill. It was our new place to be because, although Maliah no longer worked at the strip club, Murk said he couldn't go back there after he'd messed around with some broad who had worked with her.

"This is why the fuck I'm still single," he continued, throwing his hands in the air. "I met this chick…fine as fuck with thick thighs, fat ass…she ain't got no titties but I can work with that shit. Anyways, I picked her up and shit so we could go out. Why the fuck she got an attitude because I ain't wanna pay for her to get a babysitter?"

"What?" Dame grunted as he inhaled the blunt. "What da fuck her shorties gotta do with you?"

Quan over bug-eyed as he nodded his head in agreement.

"That's what the fuck I'm tryin' to say! She act like I laid down and helped her make them nappy-head ass lil' girls! Naw, I ain't gone lie… they cute but, hell…they ain't mine!" he complained, pointing his finger to his chest. "So I took her ass out, she ordered the most expensive shit she could. I wasn't even trippin' over that shit though! I ordered a side salad because I'm thinkin' 'shiiid, for $90 a plate, whatever the fuck she orderin' must be enough for the both of us!'.

Tell me why the fuck did they come back with this lil' ass piece of bird meat, asparagus, one damn carrot, and a small ass potato with some creamy shit sprinkled over the top of it? I nutted the fuck up in that muthafucka. Cussed her and every muthafucka breathin' out in that shit."

Quan finished speaking and then threw his body back in his seat with his arms folded as he pouted about his money spent.

"Nigga, you buggin'," Murk replied as he laughed at Quan's expense. "How the fuck you gone take a bitch out for something to eat and then think your ass gone eat off the same damn plate? Cheap ass muthafucka."

Quan shot Murk a sideways look and I couldn't help but laugh my damn self. How the hell Quan was so cheap when he had so much money was beyond me. He had to be sitting on a few million dollars, because his ass didn't spend any of the shit he made in the street. Even the car he drove was actually mine, and he moved into my old spot after I copped the new crib for Shanecia. He didn't buy shit.

"She should be glad I took her ass somewhere after she acted the fuck up because I didn't give money to the babysitter! The babysitter was her fuckin' friend anyways, so she was really trying to run game because she should have been watching them jits for free!" he reasoned, still seething mad as he recounted the night. "Chicks want you to take them out *and* pay for the babysitter?! Who the fuck does that shit? I'm a 'Netflix and Chill' nigga from now on. We gone watch a movie and hang out at the crib from now on and I bet not hear shit about it."

"Can't do that shit either, bruh. It ain't safe," Murk piped in. "Li got on my case the other morning talking about I don't take her ass nowhere. So after I left from meetin' up with y'all niggas, I took her to Popeyes and she got a damn attitude and told me to take her somewhere 'nice'. But all she eats is chicken and fries! I broke bread and took her to a nice ass spot downtown only for her crazy ass to order what?"

"Chicken and muthafuckin' fries!" Quan and Murk said in unison. They laughed out loud and dapped each other up. They were really on one.

"Y'all niggas stupid," Dame grumbled as he toked on his blunt. "I'm still working on getting my baby back but I know when I do, I ain't takin' Trell's ass to no damn Popeyes or splitting a fuckin' plate with her. Y'all better learn how to treat a real woman before you lose her."

The last part of his words stung me as soon as they passed through my ears. That's what had happened to me. I'd loved and lost. Only temporarily, is what I told myself…but still, she was gone.

Since the day Shanecia decided to leave, I hadn't called or texted her. As much as I wanted to pretend that it wasn't fucking with me, it was. I'd even Googled all this silly shit online to see how long it took before you could forget about a person.

From what I'd seen, it took 21 days to break a habit so I had about one more week before I could stop reaching out to squeeze her booty whenever I slept in my own damn bed. It was fucked up the things that you actually missed about a person once they were gone.

My issue was that I hadn't really come to terms with the fact that she was gone. As much as I said it, it wasn't reconciled in my mind. I felt like at some point that she would contact me and once she did, our separation would be over. I was sick of waiting on her to make a move. If I had to wait too much longer, I was just going to pop up on her my damn self.

"How is it working out with that nigga Jhonny?" I asked, changing the subject.

"That nigga bringin' in so much money, I'm thinking that Alpha might have been doing under the table deals for himself, to be honest," Murk said, shrugging.

Using my finger, I drew a line across my upper lip as I thought about that. He was probably right. At the same time, I couldn't focus on that shit.

Snatching Mello's wife had been a bust. Once word got out that we had her, turned out that nigga didn't even give a single fuck. He'd learned the day before that she was cheating and actually was grateful to us for solving his problem by snatching her and busting a cap in the nigga who she'd been fucking. Word was he'd been planning on coming back in town to deal with her ass personally, but we saved him from having to do it. Imagine that…we'd actually done that muthafucka a favor.

Jhonny got rid of the wife for us and now I was back on the hunt for Mello. In actuality, he wasn't a real problem because he was no longer in my city anymore. His niggas weren't even really pushing weight worth worrying about. But the fact that he'd touched my girl meant that I had to get rid of his ass regardless. Especially now with her tripping. She wouldn't feel safe with him still on the street.

"I want a recount on all the money, but I want you three to do it personally. If any trap comes up short, I want to hear about it and I will deal with it myself. We good on weapons?"

Dame leaned up and nodded his head.

"Yeah, I reached back to our old weapons connect at the police department in Ft. Lauderdale and he was more than happy to be doing business with us again. They confiscate enough shit from the streets to supply a fuckin' army," he informed me with a grunt.

"Well, we're about to be that army. Quan, what's up with Quentin?" I asked through gritted teeth.

Shifting uncomfortably, Quan took a minute before he let his eyes reach mine.

"He's recovering from the surgeries. And he's back on the medication the facility he was at, had him on. Legend, if you just speak to him then you'll see that it wasn't him. The medication got his mind right and—"

The more Quan tried to plead his case to me about Quentin, the more agitated I got. I was glad he'd picked up on it and closed his mouth.

"The only reason that muthafucka is still alive is because of you,

Quan," I reminded him. "But we don't have anybody but us in this world and we have to trust each other. So I'm going to trust that you can deal with your brother."

Looking me straight in my eyes, Quan nodded his head but the look in his gape was clear. He respected me and loved me as his brother and the leader, but he wasn't backing down on speaking up for Quentin. It pissed me off to the fullest but I couldn't blame him. The closest I had to a twin was Murk and if Quan's bond with Quentin was anything like ours, it made sense. No matter what Murk did, if I thought that he could be helped, I wasn't giving up on that nigga either.

"Once he gets well enough to go, I'm sending him on his way myself," Quan assured me. But it wasn't enough.

"You have until the end of next week. By then, he needs to be, not just out of the city, but out of the state. And if he ever comes back... you know what's up."

With a grim expression on his face, Quan nodded his head. Then he lifted his index and middle fingers to his lips, kissed them and patted them twice on his heart. It was something we used to do when we were younger to signify a promise made.

"I got it, and this time I swear I won't stand in the way if he doesn't listen."

Finally releasing him from my gaze with a nod, I turned to Murk who seemed uninterested in the conversation between Quan and I. I knew why. He still held the belief that Quentin should have been killed. He didn't agree with what I chose to do by letting him go free, but he wouldn't say anything against me.

Murk was merciless and, when it came to certain shit, he had no understanding at all. But I never mentioned to him about how he still dealt with Maliah after the foul shit she did, so I knew he wouldn't say a word to me about Quentin.

"Dame…how's Cush?" I asked.

My sister had been heavy on my mind since Dame had grabbed her to take her to the airport. She wouldn't talk to anybody but him at the moment but I wasn't surprised. Although she was protective of me when it came to how I dealt with my personal life, Dame had always been her favorite. Mainly because he was the big brother who always gave her whatever the hell she wanted. It bugged me that she wouldn't answer my calls but would speak to him, however, I had other shit to occupy my time.

"She's good. Got a new spot and I make sure to check in with her every night. I got one of our men up there watching her. She don't know it but I couldn't risk her being fucked with while we're still lookin' for Mello," Dame told me and I nodded my head in agreement.

"A'ight, well speaking of Mello, we got some people to run up on. We gotta find this nigga and get rid of his ass. So let's go," I told them and we all got up and started to move. It was time to get to work.

Taking up the rear, I pulled out my phone and stared at the picture of Shanecia that I had saved on the lock screen.

I'm doing this all for you, I said to her image before I pushed the phone back into my pocket.

Stepping out into the daylight, the sun burned my eyes but it barely bothered me because my thoughts were on my baby. I didn't want to admit it but I wasn't too far from picking up my phone and begging her to come back.

"You miss her, huh?" Murk asked.

I looked over at him and noticed that he'd been staring dead in my face. How he knew I was thinking about Shanecia, I didn't even have to ask. It was probably written all over me.

"Hell yeah. I don't know why the fuck she would choose to do some shit like she did but I'mma get her back."

"You showed her too much," he told me. "I don't tell Maliah shit about what we do. She knows but if I don't talk to her about it or show her, then it isn't real to her. That's how chicks think. Neesy saw too much shit."

Nodding my head, I thought about what she'd said about not wanting to be my ride or die bitch. She wanted to be my lady but, it was true, she didn't want to have anything to do with what I did. I had to rethink things because I'd always felt like when I got a woman, she would be the Bonnie to my Clyde. But Shanecia wanted something different and I couldn't blame her for that.

"Nigga, how you got to be so damn wise 'bout this female shit?" I joked, laughing a little as Murk shrugged.

"I'on know shit about women, nigga. I'm finding this shit out as I go through it. Maliah's ass be takin' me through it so, trust, I don't know shit."

Laughing, I jumped in the car and drove off. He was absolutely right. When it came to women, none of us niggas knew shit about them.

*****

The week had been productive and we'd inflicted terror the way that we were used to doing, but still no one had said shit about Mello. Not anything worth using anyways. Driving through the hood, I saw the excitement in the eyes of everyone as they watched me swerve through while staring and wondering if I was going to stop and post up with them. But this wasn't the time for that. I had other shit to tend to.

Before heading to the house to take a quick shower only to leave back out, I took a quick stop somewhere I'd been to, too many times in the past few weeks.

"You want the same one that you always get?" Belisa asked me with a smile and I nodded my head.

"I'mma get fat as hell eatin' all these damn cupcakes," I told her as I watched her grab the type I always got for Shanecia.

"From where I stand, you don't have anything to worry about," she replied with a wink. I cut my eyes at her and licked my lips. Just that quickly, I saw her go weak.

Since Shanecia had been gone, I found myself in Belisa's bakery more than I had before she left. I didn't know if it was because the cupcakes made me think of Shanecia or if it was because I was thinking of making a move on Belisa.

When it came down to it, I knew there wasn't shit I was going to do with Belisa on the long-term. I didn't want her to be my chick. But I did want a professional female that I could deal with to get my needs tended to. My dick was beginning to feel the type of distress that came about when you were used to the best kind of pussy and it was taken away from you. I couldn't get who I wanted at the moment, but Belisa seemed to be able to make a good runner-up.

"What you got goin' on tomorrow? You gone let me take you somewhere?"

I ran my eyes over her in a quick fashion before bringing them back up to pierce back into hers at the conclusion of my statement. I wasn't worried about whether or not I was dishing out good game or not. It was obvious that I already had her, so there was no point in really trying all that hard. All I really needed to do was seal the deal and I'd be on my way to what I wanted.

"Whatever you have planned, I'll be free," she enthused, her lust-filled eyes excited by my proposition.

Reaching out, I grabbed her phone from the counter beside her and pushed my number into it before pressing the call button. She grinned the whole time as she carefully followed my movements. Placing the phone back in her hand, she swooned when my finger ran along the palm of her hand and I knew then that I had her.

"Send me an address. I'll call you right before I'm ready to swing through."

Throwing a ten-dollar bill on the counter, I turned around and walked out with my mind already on the next thing I needed to do. I'd sealed the deal on a nice distraction for the meantime, so it was time to move on to the next thing on my list.

Chapter Eight

SHANECIA

Of all places to have her birthday party, Maliah decided to have it at the damn strip club. It seemed like no matter what, she couldn't stay her ass out of it. She has invited all of her stripper friends to her party and it seemed like although they weren't working, none of them knew that shit. There was ass and tits hanging everywhere. Some of them were even offering lap dances.

As I watched Maliah prance about like the queen of the world, I couldn't help but feel proud of her for how she'd turned her life around in such a short time. She'd gotten rid of Danny, made her own money, and set herself up to the point that she made her downfall her blessing. She used to have to dance at the club to make ends meet. Well, now she was renting that bitch out to celebrate her birthday. She was a new kind of woman in only a few months.

Sitting down at the table, I watched her and Murk at the bar. They were so in love to the point that I had to look away. As much as Maliah complained about all the things that made Murk different from anyone she'd been with, it was obvious she loved them all.

"Ti-Ti!" Shadaej shouted as she ran over to where I sat. Smiling, I scooped her up and sat her down on my lap. Her hair was pulled up in one of the prettiest styles I'd ever seen it in. Maliah did her thing with the girls' hair but the stylist Murk paid to come do all of their hair, including Maliah and her mother's, was *the truth*.

Reaching up, I touched my mess of curls and wished that I had straightened my hair out instead of deciding to go all natural. I was still cute and, in my mind, bad as could be, but it still was distinctly different from how I'd worn my hair all summer. In Atlanta, it was all about the natural styles and I felt comfortable enough to show my hair in its natural state: thick and curly.

"I love your hair, Ti-Ti," Shadaej cooed as she reached up and tugged on one of my curls, making it spring to life.

"Thank you, Sha," I replied with a smile and kissed her cheek. She stirred under my kiss and giggled with glee. The innocence of children. She was happy and carefree, just as a child should be.

"Are you enjoying your mama's part—"

My words cut off when I felt something in the room shift. Although I was still looking down into Shadaej's joyous face, there was a stirring in my chest and, at that moment, it was like I knew. There was no need for me to see him or for anyone to tell me. I just knew Legend was in the room.

With my lips parted slightly, I looked up, my eyes instantly falling on the place near the entrance of the club. My behavior mirrored many, as everyone shifted around to turn their attention to the source that commanded it near the front of the club.

It was him.

My heart leaped in my chest as I looked at Legend. Perfection of a man. A man of perfection.

He was simply dressed, as if not to steal the show which he couldn't possibly *not* do, with a pair of black jeans and a short-sleeved, black designer shirt that seemed like it was made just for him. His arms were exposed, showcasing his array of tattoos that completely covered his arms down to the edge of his diamond studded wrists. His hair was cut to perfection and his sideburns and facial hair seemed to be landscaped by the gods.

There was nothing about him not to love, and every eye that fell on him was instantly caught up in the rapture of him. I was instantly caught up in him. My eyes danced around every single sexy feature that I'd missed every single day of the three weeks since I'd been gone. My body betrayed me and so did my heart. They both begged for him; begged me to place Shadaej down in the chair so I could go jump in his lap, lay my head on his chest and promise him that I was there to stay.

That's until I saw *her.*

Her was the woman next to him who had her beautifully manicured, red-painted fingers laced under him where they rested on his forearm. She was very dark chocolate in color, standing next to him in a way that looked every bit of what one would call 'a black queen'. I'd seen her before but I couldn't place where. She was dressed up and looked different from how she had before.

Her natural hair hung down her back in soft curls that put my own beautiful coif to shame. Her teeth glistened pearly white as she smiled wide, comfortably accepting all of the attention that her presence next to Legend brought about. They walked casually through the crowd, greeting people as they took each step while also shattering my heart.

"Ti-Ti, what's wrong?" Shadaej's voice seeped into my consciousness, tearing my attention away from the source of what was causing it pain.

"I—I—"

I was totally at a loss for words as I looked in her soft, sad eyes that showed the empathy she felt for me. It was in that moment that I understood the error many made when they spoke to a child like the child was their best friend, aging them far beyond their years with knowledge of love lost, angst, and pain they'd never felt and couldn't possibly understand. Because, in that moment, I needed a friend so badly that I was nearly desperate enough to respond to Shadaej and tell her something she wouldn't be able to fathom in many years.

Ti-Ti's heart is broken.

Ti-Ti is devastated.

Ti-Ti wants to die.

Thank God for Maliah who saved me from reaching another level of shame.

"Sha, go find your sister. I need to speak to Ti-Ti," Maliah said as she walked up to where we sat.

Eyes wet, I wasn't able to look her in her face.

"You need to get up so we can go to the bathroom and fix you up," Maliah said in a hushed tone but still in a way that let me know without looking that she was speaking through her teeth. "This nigga just tried some bullshit bringing that bitch to my party, but I will not let him have you over here looking defeated. Get up!"

Wiping the tears from my face, I kept my head bowed as I took her hand and stood up. I bit my lip and willed myself not to look at Legend as she pulled me to the door. I was almost to the point of success…until I failed.

Over the music, I could have sworn I heard my name, although it was impossible to over the noise, and I lifted my face. At the exact same time as Legend's, my eyes swooped through the crowd and focused right on his face. In an instant that felt like hours, I saw his expression change through three swift emotions: shock, hurt, and then the last one, fear.

"NEESY, WAIT!" he yelled and took off towards me, pushing people out of his way as he moved forward.

"Oh shit," I heard Maliah curse before she dropped my hand. "This nigga 'bout to lose his damn mind."

As if in a trance, I was still focused on Legend who had took off so suddenly that he hadn't given the woman with him time to adjust. With her hand still wrapped around his arm, his sudden movement pitched her forward, making her fall over, almost tumbling to the ground if Dame hadn't been close enough to reach out and catch her. Legend wasn't the least bit moved and her near fall did nothing to break his stride.

"Neesy!" he shouted again, this time pulling me out of my trance.

I winced and became aware of the tears that were running down my face. Turning on my heels, I broke my gaze away from his face, his eyes flamed with an emotion that I couldn't yet read and his eyebrows curled in frustration. Or maybe it was determination? I couldn't tell, but I had to get out of there. And fast.

Whipping past Maliah, I cut into the bathroom and slammed the door behind me before leaning on it. Stupid plan. Where the fuck was I going to go from there? Two seconds later, Legend was beating on the door so hard that I jumped back off of it.

"Neesy! Open this muthafuckin' door!" he yelled which only made my sobs become even more uncontrollable.

"LEGEND, STOP!" I cried out in distress although I knew it was for no use. He would not stop. I knew it and so did he.

Dropping down, I sat on the floor, wrapped my arm around my legs, and cried into my knees, as he continued to beat on the door. The music continued outside but I knew no one was paying attention to that damn party. Legend was creating a scene and he didn't seem to care the least bit.

"NEESY! OPEN UP THIS MUTHAFU—Neesy," he said suddenly in a calm but pleading voice. "Neesy…baby, please open the door. Baby, open the door…please."

"GO AWAY!" I yelled as I covered my ears.

I just needed a second to myself in my own thoughts so I could get myself together, then I could talk to him. I needed a minute to get myself together after seeing the woman he'd replaced me with. That's all I needed and it wasn't an unreasonable request. Why couldn't he just give me that?

"Baby, please…" he started back again in a tone that almost shattered my will. "Please, I just wanna see you, baby."

"Legend…nooooo!"

Before I could barely get the whine out, he came back hastily with a thunderous boom, shedding his panty melting tone into the commanding growl that gave him his reputation in the streets.

"NEESY, I AIN'T GOIN' NO MUTHAFUCKIN' WHERE! OPEN UP THIS FUCKIN' DOOR BEFORE I BREAK THIS BITCH DOWN!"

The grit of his voice scared me, making me gasp. Kicking furiously, I backed quickly away, my back hitting a stall door. Then I heard Maliah's voice next.

"Uh…Legend, just maybe give her a minute to—"

"Murk, I swear to God—Murk—man, get yo' female!" Legend warned. I heard some low muttering and I knew that it was Murk pulling Maliah away. Then came Legend, issuing his final threat.

"All y'all back the fuck up! If anybody touch me, I'm shooting anything moving in this bitch! NEESY, OPEN THE FUCKIN' DOOR!"

Moment of peace officially ruined. He wasn't going to give it to me. Legend was at the point where he sincerely gave zero fucks about anything beyond what he wanted.

Standing up, I wiped my face before pulling the lock open. Before I could barely remove my hand from the door, Legend stormed in, making me jump out of the way as he slammed the door closed behind him. The rage in his eyes cooled down to a mild simmer as his eyes fell on me. He reached out to grab me but I backed away.

"Neesy, don't do this," he uttered as he looked me over, his eyes inspecting every part of me as if he'd been waiting every bit of forever to be able to see me.

"You came back."

He reached out again, but I snatched away as fresh tears came to my eyes.

"I didn't come back for you!" I told him through my tears. "And I'm glad I didn't. You've already found somebody to take my place, huh?"

Confusion laced his eyes for a beat as if he couldn't understand what I meant by my words.

"Somebody to take your place? Neesy, nobody can take your place."

"Then who is that chick you had on your arm?" I battled back.

His eyes widened with realization before dimming once more. He shook his head but kept his focus on me. I wanted him to look away. Staring into his eyes was too intense but I wasn't the one in the wrong and I was furious. I'd be damned if I was the one to back down.

"That's *not* your replacement," he replied coolly. "And I'm not tryin' to make her your replacement either. She's nothing to me. Neesy, don't do this shit."

Looking at him, I could barely believe what he was saying. He was the one who showed up with someone else. He'd moved on so easily while it was still a struggle for me every day. I couldn't even move my *thoughts* past him long enough to even entertain the idea of another man, but here he was, dating and all.

"Well, who is she?" I asked breathlessly, realizing for the first time that I'd been holding my breath. That's how bothered I was...I'd stopped breathing. Less than a few minutes around Legend and he was tapping on every emotion I had within me. The effect he had on me was incredible and sometimes I loved it but, right now, I definitely hated it.

Shifting to the side while managing to still position himself a little closer to me, Legend took a deep breath. It was cool and minty against my skin.

"She's from the cupcake shop. The one you like to go to. I just asked her to come to the party with me. That's it..."

"Have you had sex with her?" I asked him, unsure if I really wanted to know the answer.

A shadow of guilt passed through his eyes and it pierced me straight through the heart.

"You did..." I whispered out as if it was all I had left in me.

"No, I didn't!" Legend shot out. "To be honest, I wanted to but I didn't...yet."

Tears came to my eyes once more as I frowned at him. For whatever reason, he felt like telling me he hadn't slept with her yet was supposed to make everything less painful but it really didn't.

"What you expect, Neesy? I'm a nigga and I love sex but that's all it would have been. Plus, you left me anyways! Broke up with me and then planned on leaving for Spelman without telling me a thing!" he stopped and his eyes washed over my face. A single tear ran down my cheek and I watched him as he followed it all the way down to where it dripped off my chin.

"But fuck all that…I didn't do anything with her. I don't even care about that chick, she was someone to pass the time. And now you're here…" He said that last part as he looked over my entire face as if for the first time.

Using his lean but toned body, he pushed me back against the wall and I allowed him to. I took a sudden deep breath when I felt his lips on my neck, kissing me gently. Placing my hands on his chest, I nudged him away softly, not hard enough for the touch to even matter.

Chuckling in a low tone, Legend batted my hands away and then grabbed both wrists in one of his massive hands and pinned them to the side. Using his other hand, he reached down under my dress and started running his fingers through my folds. As much as I wanted to pretend that he didn't still have the same command over my body that he'd had once before, my body betrayed me and gushed out my love juice all over his fingers.

"You want me to stop?" he whispered against me, the cool feel of his breath a wonderful reprieve to my warm skin which seemed to grow hotter by the minute. He was taking me straight to ecstasy with each stroke of his fingers; the power to bring me what I needed was literally in his hands. Biting my bottom lip, I shook my head 'no'. The last thing I wanted was for him to stop. I needed this.

As soon as I answered him, I heard a soft chuckle escape through his lips. He removed his hand from under my skirt and, before I could even open my eyes to see what he was up to, he'd flipped me around, still holding my wrists in his one hand. He raised his arm up so that he was pinning my arms above my head and used his other hand to undo his pants.

By this time, I was loudly panting in desire, waiting and anticipating what was about to happen. I couldn't stop him if someone paid me to. Grabbing onto one of my ass cheeks, he pulled it slightly, just enough to push himself in. He went in easily because I was soaking wet.

"Don't ever pull that shit on me again," Legend told me in my ear as he pushed roughly into my folds. "Don't leave me again."

I won't, is what my mind said. But I still wasn't sure.

So even after experiencing the best sex I'd ever had with the only man I'd ever loved, I still knew things couldn't stay the same. After it was done, he left to take the girl from the bakery to her place with promises that he'd return to get me and take me where I belonged... home with him.

But the more I thought about it, nothing had really changed. So I grabbed a cab to the airport, waited for my flight, ignored Legend's texts and calls, and by the morning, I was back in class in Atlanta. Exactly where a girl like me belonged.

Chapter Nine

SHANECIA

Two painfully long weeks later...

The murder rate in Miami was at an all-time high. Legend was showering the city with his pain. He was making Miami bleed the way that his heart bled for me...the way mine bled for him. Nothing could stand in the face of his wrath and, even in the midst of experiencing my own heartache, I could feel his pain.

But what he didn't know is that his fury was pushing me further away.

"Captain, what are you going to do to decrease the murder rate in the city? Should the citizens of Miami be scared?" the reporter asked on the television as I looked on.

The situation that Legend had created was so horrific that it was being covered worldwide. In less than two weeks, Legend had made Miami the new Chicago. And, from the sound of it, he was becoming more and more careless about what he was doing. The bodies of his enemies weren't being tucked away and hidden as they'd been in the past. I knew it was a cry for help. He wanted me to come back but he didn't realize he was going about it the wrong way. The destruction, the killing, the horrific things he did…I just didn't want that. I didn't want to live in that kind of world.

Or did I? If I were honest with myself, I'd have to admit that I had no issues with Legend's lifestyle or what he did as long as *I didn't have to be part of it.* As long as I didn't have to see it or worry about my safety on the daily, I couldn't say I was morally affected about how he chose to live his life.

"I can assure the people of Miami that you have nothing to worry about. Yes, there is a sudden increase in gang-related activity but my team is on it and we are doing everything we can…" the police captain said.

I rolled my eyes at his statement. As soon as I saw his name run across the screen, I knew he wasn't about shit. His name was one of the ones on the checks Legend had asked me to mail off that one day. He was already on Legend's payroll. He was catching a lot of heat because of what Legend was doing, but he had no way out. He was in much too deep.

"That's some crazy shit they got going on down there, huh?" my roommate, Alani said as she walked into the living room, chomping on an apple, with her long hair pinned up into a messy ponytail held with two chopsticks.

She was a beautiful girl; she looked Black with a hint of Chinese, possibly on her father's side since she didn't know who he was. It had only been a week since she moved in but, so far, she was the perfect roommate for me because she was quiet, cleaned up behind herself, and she didn't eat my damn food. I'd placed an ad on Craigslist for a roommate and she answered it the first day. I replied back and later on that day, she stopped by with a few of her things and her money in hand.

"It is," I said as I picked up the remote and changed the channel. "That's why I left. I can't deal with all of that."

Dropping the apple on the table, she turned towards me and tucked her legs up underneath her on the couch. I glanced at her and saw *that look* in her eyes. That probing look that someone gives you right before they get ready to dive all up in your business.

"So you got a boyfriend or somebody that I can expect to see round here?" she probed. "I just wanna know if I'll be walking in and seeing some grown ass man walking around one day."

Looking down, she poked at her red and white painted fingernails absentmindedly as she waited for me to answer. She was a very proud Delta. Although she spared the main areas of the house, her room looked like a haven for her sorors and was covered with everything red and white, photos and statues of elephants everywhere.

"I don't have a boyfriend so you have nothing to worry about." For some reason, saying it aloud stung my throat. The words were sour to taste, like the vilest lie. But I didn't have a boyfriend anymore. Did I?

Alani gave me a curious look, almost as if she knew more than I was willing to say but then dropped the subject. I decided to turn my questioning on to her.

"What about you? Do you have a boyfriend?"

"Hell naw," she told me. "I'm not gonna say I haven't tried, but my sister goes through so much shit with the man she's with that I can't trust shit a man says. I'm bisexual, I guess. But, honestly, I think I might as well just say I'm a lesbian and go all the way because niggas ain't shit."

She looked at me and I saw a sparkle in her eye that made me feel like behind them she was laughing at me. Something was off with her and I started to get an eerie feeling in my chest. Like when you feel like you're the only one in the room who doesn't know something.

"But her man has been acting right lately...according to *her* anyways," she continued, rolling her eyes.

I just watched without saying a word and scrutinizing her face as she spoke each word for the hint of something else that seemed off.

"He's a major hoe...fucks everything walking and always has. Cheats on her so bad that it's a damn shame, but she has never been able to shake him until a month ago when she moved back in with our mother and stepfather. Now he claims he's a new man and he wants to be the one for her. Says he's made *progress* just because he 'ain't fuckin' no other bitches' and he's a 'one-woman man'. Have you ever heard some shit like that?"

She smiled wide and that sparkle in her eyes returned, almost as if she were beckoning for me to say the words on my mind.

"Trell? Is your sister's name Trell?" I asked suddenly. It just seemed like too much of a coincidence and I hoped that there weren't two women in the world unfortunate enough to be going through her exact situation.

Alani nodded her head.

"LaTrell...but, yes, she's my sister."

Leaning her head back on the couch, Alani let out a big burst of hot air as if letting off stress.

"You don't understand how much I've been wanting to *tell* you that, but I was told not to!"

Blinking, I tried to overcome my shock as I thought through what she was saying. She was Trell's sister? How the hell did she end up answering my ad for a roommate? Did she know me?

"How did you—"

Sensing the rest of my question before it left my lips, Alani nodded her head quickly.

"Maliah told Murk that you were thinking about posting for a roommate. Murk told Legend. They all know that I go to Clark, so he asked Trell to have me look for your ad and move in. I guess he didn't want you having some random chick living with you," Alani said with a smirk.

My head was spinning at her revelation. No matter what, it seemed like I couldn't escape Legend. I'd stopped answering his calls, blocked his text messages, and finally just changed my number altogether but, here he was, still orchestrating my life. I didn't know whether to be pissed off or happy that he still felt the need to watch over me.

"I don't mean to get all in your business—"

"Then don't," I told her with my hand up.

She ignored me like I hadn't even said a word.

"But I've never known Legend to be as in love with anyone as he is with you. I know the D-Boys are a hard pill to swallow but, even though I've only met them a couple times, I know they are good guys." She twisted up her face into a disgusted scowl. "All except for Dame."

I almost laughed at her reaction to her sister's constant mistake.

"How is Trell?" I asked, wondering about the woman I considered a friend although I'd only seen her once and spoke to her barely a few times through text.

Alani sighed and rolled her eyes. "Barely hanging on. She loves that man. She will be back with him before the month is out...I predict it."

I couldn't ignore the disgusted look that crossed her face once more, as if she were tasting something bad. A smile cracked my face before I knew it. She reminded me so much of how I'd been with Maliah when it came to Danny. I loved her ass but I was utterly repulsed by the way she always defended his ass. It wasn't until I was caught up in my own situation that I began to understand that, when it came to love, things weren't always so cut dry.

"Well, to Dame's defense, he really did a complete turnaround after she left. I am positive that he really does love her. He's working to fix his issues," I told her, honestly.

Deep down, I believed in love and I wanted Dame and Trell to work their issues out.

Alani screwed up her face, lifted her nose in the air, and stared down at me over the bridge of her thin nose.

"You should talk," she said with sarcasm. "How are you going to try to defend Dame when you're running from Legend who hasn't done half of the shit Dame has?"

She had a point, but I wasn't feeling it. She knew nothing about my relationship with Legend.

"It's not the same. Our issues aren't the same."

Alani gave me a look as if she didn't believe a word I was saying but before she could say anything, her phone chimed. Looking down, she grabbed it and started pecking away. I was grateful for the interruption.

"I need to get ready for tomorrow. I'll talk to you later," I told her in a rushed tone as I stood up and walked back to my room.

Once I closed the door behind me, I immediately pulled out my phone and dialed Legend's number but my finger hovered over the green 'call' button. Tears came to my eyes as I struggled mentally on what to do.

Chapter Ten

LEGEND

"The murder rate in Miami is at an all-time high, huh?" Quan piped up as he sat down in the chair across from where I was.

We were at what was becoming my favorite spot to the point that I'd pretty much moved in: the warehouse. I hated being in my fuckin' house because everything reminded me of Shanecia.

"Yeah, I saw Bugsy ole sell out ass on there talking about he gone crack down on it. Lying ass nigga...I wonder if his wife still got them soft ass lips. She used to suck my dick just right," Dame scowled from where he was next to Quan. "Not that I'mma try that bitch out again since I'm a changed man. But I swear I can't stand that bitch ass nigga."

Murk walked up and swatted Dame across the head. "The only reason you can't stand him is because he wouldn't let you touch his daughter. Shit...you had the mama and still was trying to get at her daughter. That's fucked up, Dame,"

"Shit, she fine as fuck...in law school and about to be a lawyer, too. She could've really helped a nigga out. Bugsy should've just taken one for the team."

Murk laughed as he sat down and started dealing out a hand of cards to Quan and Dame.

"You in on this, Legend?" he asked me.

I shook my head and Quan gave me a hard look.

"That nigga's about to get fired and we won't have to worry about his ass no more, thanks to Legend's reckless ass. I ain't never thought I would say this…but, for once, I'm scared to think about the reason you called us here tonight. Whatever the fuck you got planned really finna have Bugsy's panties in a bunch," Quan quipped as he tossed out a card.

I didn't say anything because he was right. Shanecia kept saying that she didn't feel safe. That I kept her in harm's way and that's why she'd left. Well, I was extinguishing every threat. In the past week, I'd been on a warpath for blood. I was going to flush Mello out and I was giving myself no more than a two-week deadline to do it. I was so close to getting that nigga that I could feel it, and I couldn't sleep until he was dealt with.

"Look like you got a lot on yo' mind, bruh," Murk acknowledged as he threw out a card and glanced in my direction.

"You know what he got on his mind," Dame shot back. "Me and bruh in the same boat. We missin' our ladies."

I finessed my beard and cut my eyes over at Quan who was looking at me with a smirk on his face which told me he was about to start some joking shit. He licked his lips and I shook my head to tell him I wasn't in the mood. But that didn't matter to him. He was on one.

"I have a question, Murk," Quan started, slanting his eyes at him. "How can you mend...a broken heart?" he sang out in his coarse, rough but playful tone, as he rocked his head to the tune in his head.

I blew out hot air and shook my head but, to my astonishment, Murk joined right in.

"How can you stop the rain from fallin' down?"

Lifting his hands in the air as if he was the choir director, he instructed Murk and Dame to assist him in his utter demolishment of Al Green's hit song.

"Tell me, hoooooowww can you stop the sun from shining?" they all crooned out with Quan leading the way, his massive muscular arms flailing through the air as he instructed the rest of the crew. "What makes the world go rooooound?"

I couldn't help but laugh at them. Three goons, covered from head to toe in tattoos with a combined body count higher than the population of a decent-sized city, singing Al Green to the top of their lungs. These were my niggas and I couldn't lie and say that they hadn't succeeded in lightening my mood somewhat.

"When I take care of my last problem, I'll work on getting her back," I told them with confidence. "So no more singing from you niggas."

The thing about how I felt for Shanecia was that it was beyond a simple love. I felt her in my soul. No matter how much I tried to fight her off or look up soft shit on the internet to give me a clue on how this break up shit worked, none of it worked and now I knew why.

In two months, she'd become a part of me. She was the best part of me. I was all savage and she was all beauty. She was mercy and grace. She was the part of me that had been pulled out many years before. With her, I was complete. Without her, I was destructive. But what is pure can't live where filth lies. I had some big decisions to make.

"Murk," I called out to my brother after we'd finished up discussing my latest plan to get rid of Mello for good.

Stopping just shy of walking out of the door behind Dame and Quan, he swiveled around and focused his gaze on me. Hidden behind his eyes was an expectant calm, almost like he had already been prepared for me to pull him to the side.

"What's up?"

"Chill for a minute. I need to ask you something," I said in a low tone, running my finger along my upper lip.

I wasn't even sure of the words that were about to come out of my mouth, because I couldn't even believe that I was about to say then. However, I knew that when I weighed all my options, the only ones that made sense to me were the solutions that involved Shanecia.

"You don't think I'm losing my fuckin' mind, do you?" I asked with a dry chuckle, although I was dead ass serious.

Never before had I needed anybody to cosign the things I chose to do. But when it came to this love shit, I was feeling differently about everything.

God, I need her back, I thought to myself, my shoulders drooping.

Murk laughed lightly and scratched the top of his head before he opened his mouth to answer.

"You sure you want to ask me that shit, nigga?" He continued to laugh. "You know I'm the same nigga who walked up in the strip club drunk as fuck and had a broad suck my dick just to prove a point to Maliah. As fucked up as I was about the shit that I thought Li had done to me, I still couldn't even fuck that chick to get back at her ass. That ain't never happened before."

Nodding my head, I smirked. "Yeah, I heard about that shit. Then almost shot up the damn club because some bitch tried to fight her."

"Hell yeah," he replied with his eyes pointed to the ceiling as if he was recalling the memory. "I love that girl. I'd do that shit again in a heartbeat, too, no matter how crazy it sounds because, at the end of the day, I got her back and she ain't going nowhere."

"How you know that?" I asked him with narrowed eyes. I didn't mean anything about it, I was just curious. How could he know that she wasn't going anywhere?

"Because I'll do whatever I need to do to keep her," Murk told me, his hazel eyes glowing with sincerity. "I didn't know that before, but I know it now."

Nodding my head, I reached out and dapped him up. Then something occurred to me and I decided that it was time for me to make a sudden change in my plan.

"Call off Jhonny's team," I told Murk as we walked out of the warehouse. "I don't want nobody asking any questions for me. I'm going to run the block myself and knock on every muthafuckin' door in Mello's region until someone tells me something I can use. My deadline just got moved up. I got three days to finish this nigga so I can get my baby home."

With the edges of his lips turning up into a smile, Murk nodded his head. The sheen in his eyes had shifted slightly, giving off a hungry glow, like a wild, vicious animal staring at its prey.

"I'm riding shotgun when we swerve on these muthafuckas," he told me, just as I knew he would.

"It's been a minute since I've been able to work that drum," he enthused, referring to the sound his AK made as it sounded off. "I'm ready to get this shit settled once and for all, too."

And, as if it were a sign to me that I was almost at the point of victory, a cool breeze blew along the side of my neck, where sat my newest tattoo. It was the picture of a hummingbird whose beak spelled out the most precious name I'd ever known: Neesy.

I was going to get her back and, once I did, I vowed to never let her go.

Chapter Eleven

TANECIA

It was getting harder and harder not to admit that I was falling for Darin.

"Why you pushing that shit around on your plate like that, bay?" he asked, using the nickname he'd given me some weeks before that I'd fallen in love with. "You want me to order you some food or something?"

I shook my head and dropped my fork down on the plate, making a clanging sound; at the same time a lump formed in my throat when I looked in Darin's eyes. He looked down at my plate once more and then back up at my face with his brows knitted in confusion. His cooking was perfect. Matter of fact, everything he did for me was just that. Perfect.

It had been nearly two months since the attack and I was now able to get around the house on my own with the help of a small cane. But the only reason I was even able to do that was because of Darin. In only a couple months, he'd become my lifeline. Everything I needed he supplied it and he never asked for anything in return. He cooked for me, cleaned for me, helped me learn how to walk again. He did it all. I was starting to feel like I couldn't live without him. Not just because of the way he was making me feel but because he *literally did everything*. I *really couldn't* live without him.

"What's wrong?" he finally asked the question that lingered in his eyes.

I bit my lip a little before answering. "Why are you doing all of this for me? I know you had a life before me…why are you putting everything on hold to put up with me and my…issues?" I asked, tears coming to my eyes.

The fact that I was on the verge of crying frustrated me to the fullest. I'd never been so damn emotional in my life.

I hate this fuckin' medication, I screamed in my head.

Darin's gape was wide and unbelieving. Like he couldn't believe I'd even asked him something as foolish as I had and that pushed me even closer to sobbing.

"Bay, you still don't get it, do you? I love you," he told me softly in a way that sent flutters through my entire body.

In an instance, I was a little girl again and my crush had just told me that he reciprocated my love. The tears remained but my heart was light. He'd admitted that he loved me. But how?

"How can you love me?" I asked him, a lone tear finally falling down my cheek. "What is there to love?"

"What is there *not* to love?" he asked me, his face stoic and unreadable to the point I wasn't sure whether or not I should actually answer his question.

"Tan, I've loved you since we were kids. What I have is really love…it's not that bullshit them niggas you been dealing with tell you just so they can get access to your body and your affection. You treat me like shit most the times and I've always been there for you. Even when you don't want me to. If you'll let me be your man, I won't ask you a single thing about your past. We'll start brand new…just me and you, you feel me?"

Darin's words were so touching to me that I felt like I was going to cry. The more time I spent with him, the more I realized that I didn't love myself as much as I thought I did. I was so invested in looking a certain way to cover up the insecurities about myself. Shanecia was always the smart one who did everything right and I was…well, I was always the pretty one who looked good enough to dangle on the end of a baller's arm. It wasn't that I was dumb. I was good in school; I was just better with men. I felt like there was no job that could pay me more than my pussy could make me. As much as I talked about Maliah, it seemed like everything I hated about her was everything I was.

Being with Darin showed me that it was possible for a man to love me without the bundles curled to perfection or the designer clothes and high heels. The way he looked at me hadn't changed in the least.

"I—I'm going to go take a shower," I told him, wanting to give any excuse to escape the awkwardness of our present conversation.

His shoulders drooped and he expelled a sharp sigh, so heavy that it blew a napkin clear off the table. Refusing to look at him, I grabbed my cane and stood up. As I staggered my way towards the hall, I felt his eyes on me like radiating beams. The tension in the room was thick.

Turning around, I bit my lip and, sure enough, he was there, looking right at me just as I'd known. His almond-shaped eyes were pointed down at the ends in a way that now affected me to the core of my heart. I didn't like to see him in pain.

"If you really want me…I do want to start brand new with you," I told him, finally. "I love you, too."

A smile crossed his face before he could battle it away and his lights lit up to nearly 1,000 watts. My heart swelled in my chest and I felt warm inside. For once in my life, I knew I was making the right decision when it came to love.

Sliding out of the table, Darin stood up tall, his magnificent, muscular body cloaking me in its shadow as he strode over to me with all of the confidence of a man. My man. Once he was standing in front of me, my nostrils took in a greedy share of his cologne, which seemed to be an elixir that spoke directly to my lady lips. I became wetter and wetter with each inhale.

Leaning down, he got dangerously close to my lips and I automatically lifted them towards his and closed my eyes as if he had complete control over my movements.

"I'll always want you," he whispered against my lips before pressing his soft ones against mine.

He laced his fingers around my back to support me when he deepened the kiss, and I was thankful for it because I'd completely forgot all about the damn cane. Then his hands swooped down and he lassoed his arms around each of my legs, lifting me off the floor completely so I could straddle him.

Enclosed by our passion, I wrapped my arms around his neck and pushed my tongue inside of his mouth, exploring it hungrily. Whoever said love was a drug wasn't telling a damn lie because the shit I was doing would have had my ass begging for morphine the day before, but I was just fine wrapped up in Darin's arms.

The doorbell rang and it was the only thing powerful enough to pull us away from each other. Darin slowly placed my feet back on the floor as he placed short kisses on my lips the entire way down.

"You good?" he asked me with his eyes pulled tight with concern.

Looking upwards, I did a quick assessment of my body and nodded my head. I felt great…I was hot and wet as hell but there was no pain.

The doorbell sounded off two more quick times and Darin sighed heavily as his eyes raked my body slowly. I know he was thinking the same thing I was: fuck the door, we had things to do.

Shaking my head, I grabbed my cane and nudged my head towards the door.

"Go ahead and answer it, I'll be waiting," I told him. "In the bed."

Licking his lips, he smirked and slowly nodded his head before he turned and started walking quickly to the door. I almost laughed at how he seemed to have an extra pep in his step now that he knew he was about to get some. Holding my cane tight in my hand, I went into my bedroom and washed up really quickly in the bathroom before putting on a lace panty and bra set. It wasn't the best, but it was all I could find in there. When I first moved in with Darin, he'd bought me more clothes to wear, but I hadn't picked out any lingerie. I wasn't planning on having sex with him.

After I stepped out of the bathroom, Darin still hadn't come back in the house. He'd stepped outside to continue his conversation with whoever he was speaking to and I was grateful for that. It gave me the opportunity to put some lotion on, spray on body spray, and then make his bed, to the best of my ability. After waiting for a while, curiosity got the best of me and I went to the window to peek out and see who he was talking to.

A wall partially cut off my view but I could see who it was that Darin was speaking to and it was a woman. She was fairly pretty, with warm ebony brown skin, and her hair tied up in a beautiful African printed scarf. I couldn't see Darin but from looking at her, I could see that they were engrossed in a very intense conversation. She was wearing a long, loose fitting, sleeveless gown that showed off her wonderfully toned arms but covered much of her shape.

She's pretty, I thought as I watched, feeling a pang in my chest as I watched her wipe tears from her eyes. She must have been an old flame and Darin was telling her what was up.

Backing away from the window, I sat down on the bed and wondered to myself if I had anything to worry about. He seemed to be cluing her in on the fact that she was no longer needed, so I surmised that all was well as soon as he got rid of the past so he could move on to me, his future.

Then, suddenly, I heard the door open so I hurried and laid down, pushing my cane down to the side. Darin's heavy footsteps could be heard trudging down the hall just as I got situated in the middle of the bed.

Shit, I thought to myself as I ran a finger along my lips.

I'd forgotten lip gloss. But it was too late.

When Darin walked into the room, I immediately knew something was wrong. His face was pulled into a frown and his skin was reddish in color as if flushed. Crinkling my eyebrows, I frowned as well and pulled my body up on my elbows.

"What's wrong?" I asked him.

My heartbeat was speeding up in my chest as I tried to think of the various possible reasons for why Darin was looking defeated and devastated. I knew it had to do with the woman but why was he affected in this way?

Clearing his throat, he opened his mouth to speak and my heart stalled as I waited for his words.

"Before you moved in here I was dating a chick. Her name is Jenta...nothing seriously...we were only casually dating. I met her at my gym." He paused and sighed heavily then ran his hand over the top of his head in distress.

"When I had you move in here, I broke it off with her. She was cool with it because, like I said, it wasn't serious. But that was her at the door."

He stopped speaking and it was at that moment I realized that my mouth was partially open and my throat was dry. I was waiting for the punch line because I knew it was coming. There was something with this other chick that Darin was about to tell me that would have me looking just as downtrodden as he was, and I was ready for him to spill it out.

"Okay…what? So she showed up and…?" I pushed him with my eyes wide and my hands up in the air.

"And…she's pregnant," he blurted as if it was the hardest thing on Earth for him to do. "She says she hasn't been with anyone else. She says the baby is mine."

I felt like the wind had just got knocked out of me. Falling back flat on the bed, my eyes went to the ceiling as the last words that Darin had said ran through my mind.

She says the baby is mine.

Why didn't God want me to be happy? This was bullshit. To have Darin love me my whole life and to have me looking for that kind of love my whole life, only for it to be snatched away as soon as I'm ready for it. Who does that?

As I lay on the bed wearing nothing but my bra and panties which were still moist with the lustful desire I'd felt earlier, I was hit with a strange sense of déjà vu. The last time I'd been in a man's bed, nearly naked, waiting to surprise him by breaking him off a good sample of my loving, a woman intervened and tried to kill me.

Although this time Jenta wasn't holding a gun on me, in essence she still pulled the trigger…she'd murdered whatever Darin and I *thought* we had. I knew how he felt about kids. He would try to make it work with her. He wanted a family.

Him and I would never be.

Chapter Twelve

LEGEND

The hood was happy to see Legend back on the block. I knew it was time for me to make my presence known. Even though niggas could feel my legacy every time they stepped out their front doors, there was nothing like them actually seeing you.

Murk and I were right in the middle of Liberty City on a block where a few of our boys were out serving. As soon as they saw us, they crowded around to update us on what was going on in the hood. Nothing that we hadn't already known but I let them talk anyways because it kept the moral up. After the past couple weeks of nothing but bodies dropping, it was necessary.

"You got the whole hood shook, Legend!" one of the youngest of the crew said, his tone filled with admiration. I knew him by the name of O-Town, which niggas on the block called him because he was from Orlando.

"Word?" I asked with a smile, although I already knew it was true.

"Hell yeah! You got everybody and they aunty lookin' for that nigga Mello for you, man! Muthafuckas can see that you *don't play!* You got niggas scared to even say your damn name; they on the block callin' you 'he who shall not be named' and shit!" O-Town joked as the rest of the men around him laughed.

Laughing a little, I reached out and handed O-Town the blunt that Murk and I had been smoking on. He took it happily, with a wide smile to show his appreciation of me showing that I approved of him.

Just then, I felt Murk jab me on my side and I turned towards him. He was looking to the side of us, his eyes trained on something a little off in the distance. I glanced and saw a crackhead wobbling around in the street. She looked like she probably weighed a good 90 pounds soaking wet, as she hobbled down the street wearing a short, spaghetti strap dress and flip flops with the soles missing. How the hell she managed to walk in that shit, I'd never know. The bottom of her damn feet were on the floor, she was Flintstoning in this bitch but you couldn't tell if from how she suddenly started strutting like she was wearing Jimmy Choos.

"What? You lookin' at a fiend?" I asked him when he jabbed me again.

"Look!"

He pointed and I followed his finger over to where he was pushing my attention. I looked once again at the figure, taking a longer look this time and instantly saw why he'd been trying to get my attention.

It was Boogie. Shanecia's mama. And she was high as fuck. She'd lost about another ten pounds or more since the last time I'd seen her.

She looked bad as hell. Her short hair was sticking straight up around the sides of her head, but she had a big ass bald spot in the middle. She was so damn skinny, I could see her ass bones sticking out of her damn dress. It was pitiful to look at.

"Aye, who been serving her?" I asked the men around me while keeping my eyes on Boogie.

They all turned to look at who I was talking about. O-Town laughed and then shook his head.

"Not us. We got the word from Alpha a while back when you first said not to serve her. If she getting anything, she getting it from Mello's crew somehow, because we don't fuck with her. The small few who still remain," he told me.

With my eyes focused on Boogie as she continued to stagger her way down the road, in the opposite direction of her apartment, I took off behind her. Maintaining a close distance, I followed her down the road until she dipped off into some side alley between a corner store and a laundry mat. When I turned the corner to enter the alley, I saw her squatting down, taking a piss.

Backing away, I tried to give her a little privacy but it was too late. She'd already seen me.

"Don't let me stop you," she called out in a croaky tone. "You got something for me?"

Still not wanting to look at my girl's mama peeing in the middle of an alley with her dress hiked up to her chest, I just looked away and shook my head.

"Naw," I told her. "But I might. And I got that good shit, too. But you gotta tell me where you been gettin' that weak shit you on right now."

Reaching in my pocket, I pulled out some pills, some dope, and some white so she could look at it. Instantly, her eyes lit up and she licked her lips hungrily. I knew she missed that shit that the D-Boys supplied because it was potent. We didn't do the cheap shit.

As soon as Boogie saw what I had in my hand, she fixed her clothes and stood up, absentmindedly side-stepping over the trail of pee she'd created. I fought the urge to turn my nose up in disgust as I watched her walk over to me. Lifting my hand, I stopped her from coming too close.

"It's the real deal, ma," I assured her. "Now who been supplyin' you?"

"If I tell ya, you gone give me one of them?" she asked, her eyes still on the product in my hands.

I nodded my head slowly as I let my eyes travel over her face for any resemblance to Shanecia. There was none that I could see. My baby didn't look a damn thing like this crackhead.

"I'll take you over there, but you gotta give me one of them pretty pills first," she bartered as she licked her lips once again.

"Hell naw," I replied back. "You can't hustle a hustler, ma. Tell me what I wanna hear and you get what you want."

I pulled a few of the pills out to bribe her and her eyes gleamed with desire. Suddenly, I felt another presence move in as a shadow moved in the peripheral of my eye. She saw it too and her eyes fell on something behind me. Turning around, I checked out the scene and saw it was Murk, standing some ways off in the distance with his eyes on us.

"I'm listening," I pushed her.

"Over...'bout two blocks up from here...there is a raggedy ass house next to where Ms. Lemont used to stay before she passed and her son got locked up and sent up state. The boys be cooking it over there and I knew it because I smelt it cookin'! I waited for one of 'em to come out and I asked me for some. He gave it to me and I been goin' back ever since," she finished and then put her hand over her heart as if she were promising honesty.

I knew exactly who she was talking about and it wasn't Mello's boys that were serving her. It was a group of young troublemakers that lived a couple blocks away and sold some low grade shit to a few fiends every now and then. I didn't bother them because after both of their parents were killed, the older brother began raising the younger ones. They only pushed a little amount of weight around; just enough to provide for their little family, so I didn't fuck with them.

"My payment?" she asked, holding out her hand flat in front of my face.

Exhaling, I shook my head, somewhat frustrated that I hadn't been able to get the information I'd wanted, and then placed a couple pills in her hand. I was careful not to touch her dirty ass, pissy fingers. She munched one of the pills down dry and closed her eyes as it went down, as if the high would come instantly.

Then an idea occurred to me.

"Aye, wash your nasty ass hands in that store right there and come back out. I'll have more waiting for you when you get out here," I told her.

That was all I had to say. Turning away from me, she nearly started a damn fire from how fast as her skinny ass legs ran away from me to do as I'd told her.

"What the hell you up to, Legend?" Murk asked as he walked up to me while watching Boogie run into the store.

Blowing out a long protracted sigh, I shook my head. I could barely believe the shit that I was planning at the moment.

"I'm taking her home and getting her clean," I told him. "She a dope fiend. All I gotta do is keep her away from that shit long enough to get her through the withdrawals and then throw her ass in a rehab center."

"Word?!" Murk asked me with bug eyes. "You know, you ain't never strike me as the rehabilitating type. I don't know…maybe because your ass is from the streets." His voice dripped with sarcasm. "How the hell you gone get Boogie clean?"

I didn't say anything right away. The door opened to the store and the next thing I saw was Boogie running out with wet hands and a big ass smile on her face as she eyed the place in my pocket where I'd dropped the bag of pills.

"I don't have a fuckin' clue," I admitted to Murk and he started laughing. Frowning, I turned to him and waited for his laughter to subside.

"Nigga, I don't know why you laughing," I told him. "You the one gone help me with this shit!"

"Aw, *hell* naw!"

Boogie walked up with her hand out for another pill, but I simply pointed in the direction of where my car was parked.

"Walk," I told her. "Get in the car and I'll give it to you then."

She gave me a deeply suspicious look but her hunger for more dope was much too high and overshadowed her worry. Nodding her head gently, she glanced back down at my pocket as if to make sure the pills were still there, and then took off towards the car.

And then, as if it were an omen, my phone chimed and I grabbed it out of my pocket. There was a text message from some number I didn't know. I started to ignore it but something made me go ahead and check anyways.

Legend, it's me. Neesy.

Chapter Thirteen

SHANECIA

Biting my lip, I stared down at the text that I'd sent Legend and waited until I saw the little bubbles popping up on my iPhone which signified that he was responding. My stomach was bubbling just as fast as those bubbles on my screen were moving. Why was I so nervous?

Neesy, it's me. Legend.

His smart ass return text brought a smile to my lips. Just like him to reply in that way. I rolled my eyes and then texted him again.

What are you doin'?

More bubbles. Then…

Missing you.

His reply came back fast as if it was an automatic response. Like he was saying it without thinking. My eyes filled with tears but not because I was sad. After trying to ignore it for so long, I was realizing how much I missed him too.

I don't want to speak to Legend. Can I talk to Leith?

I texted with a small smile on my face as I wondered if he would catch my drift. Legend was the man who terrorized the streets. The one people whispered about when they saw him, the fearless leader of the D-Boys. A group of brothers who seemed carefree and normal in their natural state, but turned into demons when they ran through the bowels of Miami.

But that's not who I wanted at the moment. I needed Leith. The person that Legend became when he was with me. Soft but masculine, gentle, thoughtful, loving, funny, and everything I needed him to be.

I stared down at the phone, noting that there were no bubbles. Legend probably thought I'd lost my mind. And then...

Leith? Whatchu wanna talk to that lame ass nigga for?

I couldn't help but laugh. I should've known Legend wouldn't cooperate. Rolling my eyes, I tried to fight away the smile on my face as I pecked out a reply.

I want the man who loves me.

The bubbles once again. I felt like I was holding my breath the entire time I watched them as I waited for him to reply.

No one can love you like a Legend, baby.

I nearly laughed out loud at his corny ass response. And then he continued.

All of me loves you, Neesy. The good and the bad...when you come back, I promise you'll see more good than bad.

Frowning, I bit my lip as I re-read what he'd sent me, my eyes pausing on the way he'd said when you come back and not if. Then my phone chimed once more.

And yes, I said WHEN you come back. I'm not ready for you to come just yet b/c I'm getting shit in order. But you comin' back to me. Bet ya life on dat shit.

Had I been a white girl, my face would have been all kinds of cherry red right then. This man had a power over me that I couldn't even explain. One thing was for sure…he knew me better than I even knew myself because he was absolutely right.

Even though I was sure I wouldn't when I'd initially left, I now knew that it was true. Whatever Legend asked me to do, I would do. Sooner or later, I would be back.

*****

"All I'm trying to say is that you should give him a chance," Cush pled to me for the tenth time since she'd called me only thirty minutes ago.

Sighing, I rolled my eyes and fell back on the bed. Since our talk the day I'd decided to leave and return to Atlanta, Cush and I had gotten closer and something like friends. The only issue was that we spent over half of the time on the phone with her trying to convince me that I was wrong about Legend and that I should go back.

"But Cush…you left Miami too," I reminded her. "And for the same reason as me!"

"I wasn't being totally honest," she replied with a sigh. "I have some things going on in my life that I'm not sure I want my brothers to know about just yet. After what Quentin said, I was sure that Legend would make me stay so that he could watch over me personally so…I lied and threw a fit so he'd let me leave."

I was floored. So much to the point that my mouth fell straight open. Not only had she been lying to Legend, but she'd been lying to me too.

"What on Earth could be so important to hide that you don't think you can tell your brothers?"

Silence lulled as I waited for Cush to answer my question. It was almost like the signal had died. Pulling the phone from my ear, I checked it, but Cush was still on the line.

"Hellloooo?" I sang out into the speaker.

"I don't think I'm ready to talk about it yet," she said in a rushed, matter-of-fact tone. "You know what, I gotta go."

"Wait, I—"

Before I could say another word, she hung up the phone right in my face. Dropping the phone down, I only had about two seconds to think of what secret Cush may have been hiding before my phone rang again.

"Hello?"

"Damn, Neesy, you don't know you got a sister no more?" Tanecia yelled through the phone so loud that I had to pull it away from my ears.

"Damn, Tan, you forgot how to use your damn inside voice? Heffa, you loud!"

"Listen…I have something to tell you about Darin and you can't tell *nobody*!" she started, still yelling in my damn ear.

"What is it, Tan?" I asked drily.

She was so dramatic. All this build up and she probably only wanted to tell me that Darin ironed his boxers or some random shit that I couldn't care less about.

"Darin…got a *baby* on the way!"

Instantly, a smile came up on my face. Although I was hoping that he and Tanecia would finally stop playing around enough to get together, I was still happy for Darin's news. It would be nice to see a baby around.

"Awww, tell him I said congratulations!" I told her, my smile growing the more I thought about it. "Matter of fact, I'll call him myself and tell—"

"Ain't no 'congratulations', bish!" Tanecia snapped. "I said he's having a *baby*. A surprise baby with some tramp who he was having a fling with. Ain't shit about that to be happy about."

Frowning and confused, I listened to what Tanecia was saying. What I couldn't understand was why she was so invested in Darin's personal business all of a sudden.

"Tan, why you so damn mad? What his baby got to do with you?"

Silence. The type of silence that told me all I needed to know.

"Ohhh, you *feeling* him!" I shrieked, jumping straight up off my bed. "I *knew* it would happen! I knew it! You tried to deny it, but I *knew* Darin would rub off on you! So you in love, huh?"

"Errrrrck, pump your brakes before you go planning my wedding, Neesy," Tanecia cut in, stopping my little celebration. "I told you his ass got a baby on the way. He's telling me that we can still work it out but…

how the hell am I supposed to do that with this other woman creeping around? I haven't met her and I can't stand her ass already. She always calling and updating him on shit. Why the hell he gotta know every damn thing?"

Rolling my eyes, I sighed and sat back down on my bed. For Tanecia to be the oldest, she acted so damn immature sometimes.

"Because he is the father, Tan. At least Darin is being honest and upfront with you about what's going on. He isn't trying to hide a thing. Stop hatin' this woman and you don't even know her. You know what… that's what's wrong with Black women today. Always hatin' on a sista and you don't even know her!"

Tanecia sucked her teeth. "Look at you. Every time you get back in Atlanta, it reminds you that you're Black and you start preaching again," she laughed, and I joined in with her.

"But seriously, Tan—"

"I hear you," she interrupted me suddenly. "No need to continue, Sister Souljah. I still think her ass is going to be a problem though."

"Well, wait for her ass to be a problem before you go making yourself angry."

My phone vibrated against my cheek and I couldn't ignore the way that my heart fluttered in my chest at the idea that it could be Legend texting me. Closing my eyes, I tried to calm my spirits and purposely didn't check the text.

"So what's going on with you and Legend?" Tanecia asked, as if she had gotten a signal from God that he was on my mind.

"Nothing is."

"You still aren't talking to him?"

I didn't say a word. The messages between Legend and I were a secret that I wanted to keep to myself for the moment. I didn't want to have to deal with more opinions than I already did.

"Well," Tanecia began with a sigh. "All I have to say is...if you have a good man who loves you, don't let him go...Especially, if he don't have any surprise baby mamas."

Laughing, I couldn't resist rolling my eyes once more.

"Okay, Tan. Thanks for all your wisdom. I love you, Tee."

"I love you too, Neesy," she replied back before she hung up the line.

My heart skipped a beat and I checked my messages. Sure enough, it was Legend.

You better not be entertaining them nerd niggas.

I laughed so hard at his crazy ass that I almost choked on my own saliva.

I don't know...nothing like an intelligent college boy with nerd swag, I sent back.

Smiling, I waited on him to respond but after about three minutes of nothing, I started to panic. Did I push him too far? And then the bubbles started, indicating he was replying, but I still felt anxiety about his response.

Don't get somebody fucked up.

A typical Legend reply.

Your ass just can't take a joke. That was meant to make you laugh, I texted him back while pursing my lips.

He was just too damn much sometimes and took every little thing serious. His reply came quickly.

Ok. Don't get somebody fucked up... haha

Blowing out a heavy breath, I threw the phone on the side of the bed and rolled my eyes yet again. I seriously couldn't take his crazy ass.

Chapter Fourteen

TANECIA

I'd been doing a damn good job of avoiding Darin for the last few days, but I felt like it was going to come to an end soon because he was obviously on to what I was doing. There were only so many times you could pretend to be in the bathroom, taking a shower or sleeping whenever someone knocked on your door. He was giving me time but I could tell his patience was wearing thin.

"Bay," Darin called out as he knocked at my room door. "Can I come in and talk to you for a minute?"

I shook my head 'no' but my mouth said 'yes' and seconds later, Darin had opened the door and was standing right in front of my face. I couldn't ignore how sexy and utterly breathtaking he looked as he stood in front of me in a regular old t-shirt and some shorts with sneakers.

It's crazy how thinking you couldn't have someone instantly made them everything you never knew you wanted. Darin didn't look any different than he'd always looked but now that another woman seemed to be standing in the way of me having him the way I wanted him, I was devastated.

"We talked the other night and I told you…I still want to work this out," he reminded me as if I needed it. I'd been thinking about that every night since he'd said it.

"I gave you time…but I can't wait any longer. It's awkward around the crib and, to be honest, I've waited long enough. Over ten years…" he paused and then laughed a little. "I've been waiting since I saw your ass with them lopsided pigtails ya mama put you in the first time y'all came out to the church."

He laughed a little more and I couldn't resist smiling at his comment. Yeah my ponytails had been lopsided but I thought they were the shit. And they *were*, regardless of what Darin wanted to say.

"You liked my damn lopsided pigtails," I shot back, sticking out my tongue at him in a playful way.

"Correction, I *loved* them damn lopsided pigtails," he told me as he walked over closer and then sat down next to me on the bed. "Just like I love you. I know this is crazy…the baby and all. But can we try to make it work?"

Looking into his eyes, all I felt was his love. A warm feeling passed over my body as I returned his stare but in the end it proved to be too intense so I looked away. But I knew what I wanted and I didn't want to play any games with him. I wanted Darin and if he wanted me too, I would be his. I'd be damned if I was like my sister in Atlanta, knowing damn well I wanted to be with a nigga but playing his ass and myself by acting like I didn't want what we both knew I did.

"Let's try to make it work," I told him quietly, finally able to return my eyes to his.

The most perfect smile grew on his face and it was insane to me that I could have that type of effect on a person; to simply decide to be with him and make him so happy by that one decision. Darin's entire face had lit up to the point that I began to feel like I missed something… like I couldn't possibly be the only reason he was so overjoyed.

"You just made me the happiest man on Earth," he told me.

Smiling up at him, I felt for the first time in forever that I was exactly where God wanted me to be. When Darin lowered his head and placed his lips on mine, it was the best feeling I'd ever felt. Truly perfect.

Before I knew it, he was pressing me back onto the bed and I allowed him to have his way, falling freely on the pillows behind me, ones that he'd picked out specially for me to ensure my comfort. He was thoughtful in all the right ways and about all the right things.

"I'll take it slow…if you're ready?" He lifted his head to get my consent, but I was already nodding my damn head so fast you'd think it was likely to fall off my damn neck.

I hadn't had sex in what felt like a million years and, even if I had, I was too damn ready because I could feel his massive eggplant pressed up against my leg. To be honest, I could barely *lift* my damn leg but wasn't a damn thing hard about opening my thighs. If he was good on doing all the work, a bitch was good to go!

"Ahhh…" I moaned as he shifted my body around so he could ease off my thin, cotton shorts.

"Did I hurt you?!" he asked, sitting up immediately.

"No," I replied honestly. "I'm good…just, I can't do much but—"

"Shhhh," he shushed me while shaking his head gently from side-to-side. "I got this, baby."

And he damn sure did.

Darin made love to me with the care of a man who had been waiting years to finally get the pussy…because, apparently, he had. There was something about good sex, but there was something different about having your body *appreciated* during sex. He kissed every inch of me. From my forehead to my little baby toe; even my scars from where I'd been shot. It was so sweet to me that he found beauty in the places that I couldn't even bear to look at myself.

Then his lips kissed my lady lips and he sent me on a rollercoaster ride of pleasure that I'd never before experienced.

"Oh my g—shit, Darin!" I yelled and then bit my lip to keep myself from screaming out. "Fuck!"

"Don't hold it in," he whispered, his hot breath sending tremors through my clit as he spoke. "Let me hear you moan."

And with that, he pressed my thighs further apart and dipped his whole damn face inside of me, lapping from front to back as if I was the sweetest, tastiest meal on Earth. Words couldn't even attempt to explain how he made me feel.

My body started trembling and I began to fight to get away, but he latched his arms around my legs and kept me still. Within seconds, my sweet nectar was covering his face. Cupping my ass and lifting it up to his face, he started sipping and licking from me as I continued supplying him with my honey. I was spent but he wasn't through.

Standing up, Darin reached into his pocket and pulled out a condom. I couldn't help but smile. His ass had come prepared to get some.

"Am I that damn predictable? You knew I was gonna give it to you, huh?" I teased, still holding my smile.

Darin dropped his head to the side and tossed me an uneasy smile as he rubbed the back of his neck.

"Shiiidddd, a nigga can wish for a miracle, can't I?" he asked, his smile growing brighter.

I replied without words by opening my legs wider. He got the message and licked his lips once more before placing the condom on his erection, which gave me a full view of exactly what he was working with.

Gotdamn, I thought as I looked at the anaconda he was wrapping up. *Good boys be packing big shit!*

Had I known Darin was holding like *this* I would have gave him some a long time ago. There was no man gifted like his ass, he looked like something from a porn video. Now I could see why his baby mama had gotten pregnant even with them using a condom. Wasn't no holding that monster ass dick down.

With a cocky grin, Darin stroked his dick a few times as he looked at the amazed expression on my face.

"Yeah, you see this shit," he said proudly as he began thumping it against my upper thigh. "I can do some major shit with this. You know that, right?"

Hell, I believed him.

Leaning over me, he kissed me deeply, distracting me from the anxiety that was rising up in my chest. As many men as I'd been with and my nerves were in a fuckin' wreck. I was so worried that I wouldn't be good enough and that he wouldn't be pleased with me. He had me feeling like a virgin all over again.

"I love you," he said softly as he started easing himself into me. His words instantly put me at ease. "I always have."

"I love you too," I replied back to him. "And I always will."

And just as I'd said it, I knew I meant it. As sure as the air that I breathed. I did love him and I probably always did. But, finally, I was realizing he was the one.

Dipping his head down, Darin sucked in one of my nipples as he increased his thrust a little more and pushed deeper into me. I gasped suddenly as the wave of euphoria from having a good, thick pole touch spaces that have never been explored, washed over me.

"You good?" he asked me as he started to increase his speed, pushing in and out of me in a rhythm that had me about five seconds from going absolutely insane.

"Yes, baby! Oh god…YES!" I yelled as a shiver of ecstasy travelled through me.

Tears came to my eyes. I couldn't take it anymore; the more he pushed into me the crazier I got until I was thrashing against him, turning all of the pain that I'd been experiencing before into sheer pleasure. He was knocking right on my G-spot and was about to send me into a fucking frenzy. I wanted him to stop but I wanted him to go at the same damn time. I couldn't make up my damn mind to save my life.

"FUCK!" I screamed as he continued to stroke inside of me; each stroke sending me closer and closer to my orgasm until I was finally there.

Leaning down once more, he bit down hard on my nipple at just the right moment, and I creamed all over him at the same moment that he came. We collapsed on the bed and less than a few minutes later, we were both asleep.

And then about an hour later, we were up again. Darin's phone went off and, even after he ignored the first call, whoever it was called right back, destroying sleep for the both of us. Groaning, I rolled over to free up his arm and allowed Darin to answer his phone.

"Whoever the hell that is better be on fire or dead," I slurred, still drunk over the aftereffect of our sex.

"Hello?" Darin mumbled into the phone.

I heard a woman's voice talking hurriedly, like in a panic, on the other line and my eyes shot open. It was like a double shot of caffeine. My ass was wide awake and listening hard as hell so I could catch any damn reason to go the hell off.

"What?! What happened?" Darin said, now also in a panic. Groaning, I rolled my eyes. It had to be Jenta.

He jumped up and ran to the bathroom next to my room. I heard the water come on, drowning his voice out so I couldn't hear a thing. Sitting up on the bed, I crossed my arms in front of me and pouted for a bit, even tried to push out a few tears so when he came out, I could lay the waterworks on him and get some sympathy.

It was petty but that's what I was. Petty Betty with a capital B and I wasn't about to let her call and get my man all riled up without me pulling a stunt to make myself feel like I had the one up on her ass.

Finally, I was able to squeeze out a single tear just as Darin came out of the bathroom.

"Bay," he said as he walked into the dark room. "I gotta go. Jenta called me and—"

He turned on the light and when his eyes fell on my face, he paused and then frowned.

"The hell you cryin' for?" he asked me, looking me up and down as he sized me up. "Sittin' there with your arms folded and shit too, huh?"

Darin shook his head, clicked his tongue against his teeth and then started pulling on his clothes, ignoring my tantrum completely. This was not the response I'd been hoping for.

"Tan, you forget that I *know* your ass. You not dealing with just another nigga. I know how you operate." He shot me a look as he started to lace up his sneakers. "Stop being dramatic for no damn reason. I'll be back. Jenta had a scare...some spotting and contractions...so I'm going to the hospital with her to make sure everything is alright."

Standing up, he walked over to me and rubbed the top of my head, completely messing up my hair, and then leaned down to kiss me. His lips felt cool against mine and he calmed my spirits a bit, but I was still slightly pissed off that he had to leave.

"I love you and I'll be back. Get some rest. When I come back, I might want some more," he said with a wink and then licked his lips, sending chills up my spine.

Tossing him a small smile, I watched as he walked out of the room and then listened out for the front door closing. Here I was alone in the house I shared with Darin because his baby mama had called him about an emergency. My mood had gone from the highest point to a new low all in the matter of hours.

Better get used to it, I thought to myself as I laid down on the bed. *This won't be the first time she calls and your man goes running.*

And it definitely was not.

Chapter Fifteen

MALIAH

The days were passing by and I felt like all I was doing was watching them go. School was in so the girls were gone during the day, so I spent my days tending to Dejarion and watching soap operas with my mama. That is…when her ass was home. I was still convinced she had a boyfriend that I didn't know about and I was just bored enough to take out some time to get to the bottom of it all.

"Where you went last night, Mama?" I asked as I walked right into her room without knocking. It was cracked open but I knew she was going to chew my ass out about it anyways.

"Why you askin' me about my whereabouts, Maliah? I'll tell you where I wasn't! I wasn't in yo' business so you need to A-B-C your way out of mine!" she snapped.

She rolled her eyes and poked her lips out as if she'd just given me a good ole tellin' off instead of using those old lame ass lines.

"Well, you livin' in my house and I got some rules round here," I started in a joking way as I sat down on her bed and watched her frown at me. "And one of the rules I have is that if somebody leaving out of here in the middle of the night with her makeup done and a hoochie mama dress on, I need to know where she goin.'"

Smirking, I crossed my arms in front of my chest as she glared at me from where she sat in her Queen Anne chair next to the large floor-to-ceiling window in her room. It was her favorite spot to read the Bible during the day. Or at least she said it was the Bible. Only God and Satan knew what the hell she really had in between those pages.

Placing her current read down on her lap, she folded her arms in front of her and glared at me.

"This ain't your house, darlin.' Might I remind you of the time you had to ask me if you could stay back in your old room because somebody had changed the locks and wouldn't let you come inside?" she replied with a smile on her face.

Immediately, I began to pout.

"Low blow, mama," I replied with a roll of my eyes.

Sighing, I laid down on the bed and cupped my chin in my hands.

"But for real…you got a boyfriend?" I asked her again with a little more humility in my tone.

Giving me a small smirk while raising up one eyebrow in the air, she picked back up her Bible and placed it in front of her face.

"I have somebody who has taken interest," she stated in an even tone but with a hint of excitement as if she'd wanted to share it with me all along.

"Well, when can I meet this someone?" I pressed, unable to hide the big ass grin that was spreading across my face.

It had been a long time since my mama had been with a man. Matter of fact, since my father, I'd never known her to date anyone. She always said that she sacrificed the better years of her life to take care of me and my brother, and would complain about how much of a waste that was when we didn't 'turn out right'. But, honestly, I always felt like she didn't date because she wasn't over my daddy.

"You can't meet him right now," she said in a rushed way. "H— he's…I'm just not ready for that right now."

Immediately, the alarms started sounding off in my head. From the look on her face when she finally mentioned him, it seemed like, whoever this man was, he was more than a casual encounter but now things were beginning to seem strange. First of all, she only ever met up with him at night. Secondly, here she was talking about that he 'wasn't ready' for me to meet him.

"It's not Brother Ivory from the church, is it? I saw the way he was looking at you last Sunday when he came and picked up the collection plate," I inquired.

Yes, I was still going to church every damn Sunday. I wasn't living right but I did tell God if He helped me through Murk finding Danny in my mama's house and stopped him from killing my ass, that I would go. But God had even taken it a step further and made it so I hadn't even had sex with Danny, so I was holding up to my end of the bargain.

"Hell naw!" my mama scoffed, her nose turning up in disgust. "I wouldn't sleep with that reptile if his dick led to the stairway to heaven. I can't stand his ass!"

"Mama, you can't talk like that!" I told her in between laughing.

"You can't talk like that either! Mention me messing with that troll again and it might send you straight to hell. I'll be damned before I mess with his ass...Yuck!"

I was in the middle of laughing at her when I heard the front door open and close, letting me know that Murk was finally back. He'd been gone most of the night, saying that he'd needed to stroll the streets with Legend. Then he came back for a couple hours only to leave again right after the girls left for school.

"Well, nice talkin' to you, heffa, I know you leavin' now so you can tend to your man," my mama teased as I started to stand up.

Rolling my eyes at her, I skipped right out of the door and down the hall towards Murk. I'd been wanting to talk to him about something all day so I hoped he was in a good mood.

When I walked in the kitchen, I found him standing in front of the open refrigerator with a carton of orange juice in his hand as he drunk straight out of the carton. I sucked my teeth and watched him without saying a word. I'd told him plenty of times before that he couldn't do that nasty shit now that he didn't live by himself, but Murk always did exactly what he wanted. Either way, I wanted him to be in a good mood for what I wanted to say so I wasn't about to mention it.

"Hey baby," I cooed as I leaned against the wall and watched him.

Still gulping from the carton, he shot one eye curiously in my direction. Then he took his final swallow and removed the carton from his lips to place it back in the fridge.

"What you want, Li?" he asked as he wiped his mouth and closed the refrigerator door. "I know you hate when I do that shit, so you must want something since you actin' all sweet and shit with me."

Expelling a deep breath, I rolled my eyes.

"Why I always gotta want something, Murk?! I can't just be sweet for no reason?" I asked him with my hands out.

Murk turned around and stared at me in disbelief. He didn't say anything, he just blinked at me like I was bullshitting. Which I was.

Damn!

"Okay, fiiiiiiiinnne," I started. "I did want to talk about something."

Crossing his arms in front of his chest, Murk stood with his feet firmly planted on the floor but he didn't give me any indication as to whether he was in a decent mood or not. I began to lose my nerve for what I wanted to ask and started shifting from foot-to-foot.

Noticing my anxiety, Murk let out a breath and then pushed past me as he began walking towards the hall.

"Whatever it is, I can tell I don't wanna hear it," he muttered as he walked down the hall with me right on his heels.

"Murk, how can you say that? You don't even know what I want to ask!" I told him as we both walked into the room.

I closed the door behind us and watched him as he began to undress.

"All I want to say is that I'm bored staying at the house all day!" He let out an indignant grunt but I continued. "I want to work or something. Can't I go back to the club—"

Murk snatched his head up so fast and glared at me so intensely that I thought I was going to spontaneously combust into tiny pieces.

"No! Not as a stripper! As a bartender or something! They make just as much money…but it's not even about the money. I'm just tired of being home all day…I wanna do something!" I voiced in desperation as I watched him begin to grow angrier and angrier by my plea.

Kicking off his boots, Murk walked towards me with a deep scowl on his face. I'd picked the wrong damn time. His ass was mad as hell. I don't know what the hell had happened in the streets the night before, but he wasn't in the mood for anything I had to say.

"Why the fuck you always wanna be somewhere shakin' your ass and shit?!" he started.

"But I don't wanna strip! I said that—"

"I don't give a fuck what you *said*! Listen to what da fuck I'm sayin'! HELL NO!" Murk roared. "You wanna get out there and pour drinks and shit for the same niggas who used to run their hands through the crack of your ass, and you think they not gone try to do that shit again just because you ain't on a fuckin' pole?!"

I hadn't thought about that part and I had to admit he was right. It didn't matter what the hell I was wearing, my customers at the club were used to seeing me naked and they only looked at me like a piece of meat. Wasn't shit going to stop them from expecting they still had certain rights to my body.

"But…I'm just so tired of sitting around this house all the time! All I do is take care of the kids, cook, clean, and watch TV and shit! Why can't I do something?" I began to whine.

"You *can* do something!" Murk finally told me, giving me a small sense of hope. "Take your ass down to that school that the girls go to and volunteer or some shit. Do something that involves covering your ass! Use your brain…shit, you would think all you had was a body! That's my body! That pussy, them titties, that ass…all that shit is *mine*. Stop thinkin' you can just show your body to these niggas and I'll be fine with that shit!"

My lips parted slightly in shock at what he was saying but also in desire. He was shooting me some real shit…some real shit that I hadn't even considered, but it was speaking to my mind and my lil' lady between my legs who was gushing from what he'd just said.

That pussy, them titties, that ass…all that shit is mine, I repeated his words in my mind. *Got damn!*

"I—I…I know, I just…"

My voice trailed off because Murk started walking towards me. Before I could even consider what he was about to do, he reached out and placed his arms around my waist then pulled me into him. He caught me with his lips and kissed me deeply while he wound his erection into me. He was rock hard and ready to go. My mouth began to salivate as I felt his bulge get harder and harder.

Within seconds, we were both ass naked and he had me booted over the bed while he rammed me from behind. As he dug deep inside me, I bit down on the pillow in front of me to stop myself from crying out while he went to town all up in my pussy. Or as he'd put it, *his* pussy. He was illustrating every damn thing that he'd said before. My body was his and he was putting his mark on it, as he pushed his fingers in every hole and explored every spot on me. He squeezed hard on my breasts, kneaded his fingers through my ass cheeks like dough, pushed his thumb in my ass and thrust his dick damn near to my chest cavity.

"DAMN!" I cursed when he began throwing his dick in a circle, hitting my spot just right. "SHIT!"

I couldn't hold it in. I was about to cum and from the way his pole was thumping inside of me and his strokes were speeding up in tempo, I knew he was about to cum too.

"FUCK!" Murk gritted as he finally let loose right inside me, slowly sliding in and out in a rhythmic motion as he deposited his seeds into me.

Breathing hard, I collapsed on the bed to recuperate as he pulled out of me and started to walk towards the bathroom. He ran the water for a short while and then walked out with a wet washcloth in his hand as he wiped himself clean.

Then suddenly, he dropped the rag on the floor and walked over to me, grabbed both of my ankles into his hands and lifted me so my ass was in the air.

"MURK! What the *fuck* are you doin'?" I asked him as I grabbed at the sheets on the bed to steady myself. I couldn't do shit with him holding my legs straight in the air. I was partially suspended in air, dangling from his tight grasp.

"Stop wiggling, Li!" he ordered with a light chuckle.

"Nigga, what kind of game you playin'?" I asked him as I jerked a bit, still trying to get away from him. He gripped my legs harder and shook a little.

"I'm tired of you mentioning this strip club shit so I'm makin' sure I don't hear about that muthafuckin' place no more," he told me in a playful tone.

Finally, he released my legs and the bottom half of my body fell to the bed with a thump.

"What the hell was that about?!"

Running his thick tongue across his teeth in the way I loved, he looked at me with twinkling eyes, laced with laughter, and smiled.

"I was helping my soldiers get to where they needed to go," he explained. "Now I better not hear shit else about that muthafuckin' strip club. You pregnant now."

Gasping, I grabbed a pillow and threw it straight at his head.

"MURK! I swear you ain't shit!"

Chapter Sixteen

LEGEND

"The block is hot," I said to Murk as we sat on the front stoop of Jhonny's mama's spot eating some good ass cookies that she had baked for us.

Ms. Berneice was the closest thing we had to a mama in the streets. She always kept us fed when she saw us. I loved her old ass even though I wasn't sure she knew it. I didn't hang around much and whenever I did see her, I never had much to say. But I always made sure she was good, she just didn't know it. One of the envelopes of money that I sent out each month was addressed to her, she just had no idea who it came from because I'd never left a return address.

Murk nodded his head and popped a cookie in his mouth before following it up with some milk. Suddenly, a young chick, looked like she had just turned eighteen the day before, walked by us wearing a pair of dusty looking coochie cutters and a dingy white tank top that showed off her belly complete with a big ass outie belly button. She turned and gave us what was probably supposed to be her sexy look before licking her lips and switching her ass extra hard as she sauntered away.

"Naw, my nigga, the block is *stank* and hot," Murk corrected as he turned his nose up at the chick. "I can't believe I used to give these nasty ass gutter bitches a chance back in the day."

Laughing at him, I shook my head.

"Don't be turning your nose up at that bitch," I joked. "Actin' like you too good. Hell naw."

"Nigga, I *am* too good," he corrected me. "Always been. I just didn't know my worth."

We both burst out laughing at that one. His ass was dumb as hell.

"Yo, you heard from Quan recently? I been callin' his ass but he always actin' like he up to something or some shit. It makes me feel like he still got Quentin hiding out over there."

I scratched at my jaw as I thought about the last conversation I'd had with my brother. Something was off with Quan but it was obvious that he was hiding something. What he was hiding, I didn't know but I was certain it had something to do with that twin of his.

"Naw, I ain't heard from that nigga. Ask Dame," Murk told me.

Turning to my right, I looked over at Dame who was a few paces away talking to a chick. I had to do a double take because the last time I'd looked over there he was standing alone, but now he had some googly-eyed model looking bitch all up in his face.

"Aye, he done gave up on Trell?" I asked Murk as I looked on and shook my head from side-to-side.

"Hell, look like it. But can you blame him? Shit, she been gone for months. I can't blame that nigga for wanting to get his dick wet," Murk replied as he started rolling up a blunt.

I couldn't say I disagreed. The time that Shanecia had been away had been hard as hell for me. I wasn't used to not getting tended to on the regular, whether it was during Shanecia or before Shanecia. I always had a chick I could call to come in and handle me just right before I sent her on her way. Belisa from the bakery was supposed to do just that before Shanecia showed up and blew that shit to pieces for me. Truthfully, it was a stupid idea to try to holla at the chick that sold her those damn cupcakes anyways, but I hadn't been thinking with the right head. Since then, I hadn't thought about hooking up with her or anyone else again but, now that Murk mentioned it, the itch was coming back.

"True," I replied as I took out my phone and started scrolling.

Ticara, I thought as I stopped over her name in my contacts.

Ticara was a bad ass female that I messed with a few times right before I got with Shanecia. She'd called a few times since we'd been together but I didn't answer. When Shanecia and I made it official, I cut every damn body off but I knew any of them would be happy as hell to hear from me even if it had been some months.

Aye, what's good? I texted her.

I wasn't down for waiting on a reply so I was about to put the phone in my pocket and carry on with my business, but she hit me back quick.

Ticara: *Hey baby. I missed you.*

Snickering, I shook my head as I read the text. I hadn't messaged or spoke to her ass in months and here she was with this 'hey baby' shit. But that was one of the things I liked about Ticara.

She was a professional woman, smart, had her own shit, and was bad with it. She started out in the hood doing hair on her mama's steps, but turned that shit into a huge business with multiple salons all over South Florida, L.A. and New York City. She didn't sweat a nigga because she didn't have time to, and she never thought what we did was more than it was.

You in town? Wanted to see if you could swing by.

Naw, I'm in Philly. I'll be back next weekend.

Next weekend was too damn long for me to wait. I needed this shit handled now.

Check flights, I told her. *I'll fly you in but you gotta get here tonight.*

There was nothing for about ten seconds and then…

I'll be there, baby. I'll hit you back with the info. Here's something to hold you until I get there.

Seconds later, she'd sent me five pictures of herself naked in various poses that got my dick rock hard.

Shit, I thought as I looked at them. She was one sexy ass bitch. Exactly what I needed to hold me over until I was able to get Shanecia back down here.

"Nigga, what you doin'?" Murk said from beside me.

I looked up and he was giving me a side eye as if he knew something I ain't want him to know.

"Hittin' up Ticara. Remember her?" I asked as I flashed him the picture on my screen of Ticara standing in the mirror naked with every damn thing on display.

"Hell yeah I remember her ass," Murk told me with a smile. "I actually saw her ass first but you stepped in and grabbed her before I could. That was some bullshit."

"Nigga, she was giving me the dick sucking signals for damn near thirty whole minutes before I walked over to her ass. She wasn't checkin' for you," I chuckled and tried to duck out the way when Murk punched me in the side.

"Y'all boys want some more cookies?" Ms. Berneice's voice rang out from behind us.

Shaking my head, I turned around and looked into her wrinkled, old face. She was an older woman who you could tell was drop dead gorgeous in her younger days. She had a caramel complexion and blue eyes that I wasn't sure had always been blue or just became that way with old age. Her long, thick silver hair hung down her back in loose curls, swooping from side-to-side as she approached us.

"No ma'am," Murk replied, handing her the tray of cookies. "You 'bout to make a nigga get a big ass gut round here, Ms. Berneice."

The older woman chuckled in a way that sounded like dancing wind chimes, as she grabbed the tray from his hands.

"You could stand to gain a little weight, Pablo. That girl ain't been cooking over there? I taught her a few recipes when she was younger that should get you some meat on them bones."

I fell out laughing as Murk looked at her like he was mortified.

"What you mean, Ms. Berneice?" He flexed his muscles. "I ain't no skinny nigga by a long shot. I'm still toting these guns," he said as he lifted one arm up and made a muscle. "I'll knock a nigga out on sight. One hitter quitter for sho."

Ms. Berneice giggled again as she watched Murk flex over and over again to prove to her that he still had it.

"Hell naw," I laughed as I watched him. "Nigga, get out your feelings. Ms. Berneice just messin' with your sensitive ass."

Murk's eyes swooped over to her face as if searching for confirmation.

"Is that true?" he asked with one eyebrow lifted.

She rolled her eyes and turned to walk back inside her house, balancing the tray of cookies in her hand.

"Y'all boys let me know if you need anything—"

"Aye, Ms. Berneice, where you goin' with them cookies?!" Dame called out as he ran over.

She stopped and turned around just in time for him to drop his hands right on the plate and grab up three. He gobbled down the first one and stuffed the other two in his pocket.

"I thought you were done, Damion," she told him. And then she continued with a reproachful tone. "I saw you talking to Jessie's daughter over there."

I looked at Ms. Berneice as she glared at Dame with one eyebrow lifted. Catching her drift, I smirked and grabbed up the blunt that Murk had just rolled, dancing it back and forth between my fingers.

"Huh?" Dame asked as he looked back at her while chewing on the cookie, wondering what the purpose was behind her glare.

"Yes…Jessie's daughter. I saw you talkin' to her," Ms. Berneice told him. "She's pretty."

"Oh!" Dame said, finally understanding what she was trying to hint at. "Naw, it ain't even like that, Ms. Berneice. That hoe—er, I mean, that *young lady* ain't anybody I'm interested in. She's cool with my girl and I just wanted to see if I could get her to pass Trell a message for me."

Lifting one brow up, I looked at Dame in surprise. He was actually still sticking to his word. He wasn't dealing with any other females until he was able to get Trell back.

"I don't want nobody else," Dame continued. "I made a promise to my baby…in my mind because she won't answer my calls…but, anyways, I promised her that I wouldn't deal with another chick until she came back to me and I mean that. I ain't worried about these other bit—um, other ladies."

Ms. Berneice's eyes widened as she looked at Dame in admiration and then slowly nodded her head.

"I'm proud of you, Damion," she said with a smile on her face. Then she cut her eyes to me. "And Leith, give your brother some credit because he told me you've been giving him a hard time. He's been doing a very good job waiting on his woman without yielding to temptation."

I grunted and shot my eyes at Dame who was standing with his hands on his hips, his chest out and a big ass, goofy grin on his face. He looked like a lil' nigga in kindergarten who had just won a gold star.

"Snitchin' ass nigga…" I muttered at him under my breath.

"Which is more than I can say about you," she continued in a condescending tone. "I heard you out here talking about Little Ms. Ticara."

A smile shot up on my face as I glanced at Ms. Berneice who was giving me a knowing look. She turned around to head back inside the house but, before she walked inside, she said one last thing.

"And tell her to stop sending them nasty pictures to your phone. I know her father wouldn't be happy about that. He's *still* the deacon over down at the church!"

And with that, Ms. Berneice slammed her door closed behind her.

"How the hell she be knowing every damn thing?" Murk laughed once she was gone.

"Probably because Dame be tellin' her every damn thing," I muttered. My phone chimed and I grabbed it as they continued to talk.

Ticara: *I found a flight back leaving in 4 hours. Want me to book it?*

Naw, I replied back and placed the phone back in my pocket.

If Dame's ass could hold out for as long as he did waiting for Trell, I could definitely wait until Shanecia was mine again. Wasn't no pussy like hers anyways so I would just be playing myself.

Suddenly, I had the crazy feeling I was being watched and I glanced up, allowing my eyes to move back and forth over the block as I scrutinized everything. It felt decent outside, the sun had gone down and the street lights were on. There was a nice calm breeze in the air and that's why every damn body was outside enjoying it. There was a pick-up game of basketball going on. Bad ass bitches were strolling trying to find a sponsor. Niggas were cat-calling and shit, trying to get some attention. The strong smell of loud was permeating through the air and, until that moment, I was enjoying the few moments of sitting on the block watching the activity. But now I was feeling like something wasn't right.

Standing up, I stuck the blunt between my lips and was about to light it when something caught my eye. Focusing my gaze, my teeth clenched down on it instantly when I saw who it was. I snatched the partially severed blunt out of my mouth and tossed it down to my side.

"Nigga, what da fuck did you do to the blunt?" Murk cursed as he picked it up and looked through it. "Fuck! What the hell you was tryin' to do? Eat the shit?"

"Fuckin' Quentin," I grumbled under my breath as I grabbed my strap from my side.

"What?" Murk looked up and followed the trail of my eyes. Dame stood up by my side and did the same.

There, off in the not-so-far-distance, was Quentin. He was walking towards us with a fairly quick stride and his eyes focused in on me. He had a stoic expression on his face but his eyes looked tame and didn't hold the usual wild and crazy stare that I'd gotten used to seeing in them. He placed his hands up in surrender but I didn't give a fuck. I still started to raise my piece up in the air. But then Dame stopped me.

"Naw, not in front of Ms. Berneice crib," he said and I had to agree with him.

I didn't want to unnecessarily bring this shit to her doorstep.

"What da fuck you want, nigga?" I gritted when he finally approached us.

I felt my blood turn to fire as I looked at him. The only thing I really wanted to do at that moment was silence him forever but, once again, I was being stopped from doing what I wanted to do. This shit had to stop.

"Listen, Legend, I was on my way out but I got some news that I thought you might have wanted to hear about," he started.

"What news, muthafucka?" Murk grumbled from beside me. "And you better make this some good shit because you know you ain't supposed to be 'round here."

As if to further illustrate his point, Murk pulled out his Desert Eagle and examined it one good time before dropping it to his side. Quentin watched him for a second before turning to me.

"I know where that nigga Mello is," he said. "He back in the city."

Now he had my attention.

"Continue," I told him, me, Murk, and Dame all standing at attention with our full focus on him as we waited for him to speak.

"He was out of town hiding his kids and shit. Also, he's been trying to get a new connect with product better than yours and connect with a team of out-of-town niggas since you demolished the few niggas he had working for him here. I was waiting for the Greyhound and I saw some fine bitches walking by so I went and tried to holla—"

"Get to the point, nigga," Murk pushed and Quentin gave him an annoyed look before he continued on right where he left off.

"—So I walked over but one of them gave me a stank ass look when I tried to say something to her and she was like 'Nigga, I thought you said I wasn't your type!'" Quentin shrugged. "I didn't know what da fuck she was talkin' about and thought my meds were fuckin' with me until she called me 'Quan.' I was gonna tell her I wasn't Quan, but then she told me that she had some information for me and if I would have been nice to her when we first met, she would tell me. So I talked the bitch up and shit…and she told me where Mello was. She said he living with some light-skinned female over off A1A."

Quentin smiled as if I was supposed to congratulate him or some shit but that wasn't going to ever happen.

"You got the exact address?" I asked him. He nodded and rattled it off to me from memory. I listened intently and locked it into my brain.

"Grab him and let's go," I said to Murk and Dame as I grabbed up my shit from the front stoop in front of Ms. Berneice's house and got ready to head out.

They did as I asked and Quentin didn't even try to fight them off. He was fucked up but he was blood and he knew enough about me to know how I rolled. I was about to verify his info and then I'd figure out what to do with him later.

Licking my lips as I walked over to the whip, I couldn't help but begin to get excited. As soon as I was able to get rid of this nigga, nothing would stand in the way of me getting my girl back. I was one step closer and, with any luck, hopefully this would be the final step.

✶✶✶✶✶

"You think this it?" Dame asked as we pulled up in front of the address that Quentin had given us.

It was a decent-sized brick house. Not small but a far cry from what Mello had been living in with his wife. Even smaller than what he'd had Tanecia in.

"This it," Quentin said from the back.

"How the hell you know, nigga?" Murk shot back at him.

"Because the bitch that told me about it said that the window in the back was broke and had to be replaced. She said that he was in there fucking her friend when his main bitch came back. He made the friend climb out the window and she broke the shit when he tossed her out," Quentin explained.

I looked to the back part of the house. Sure enough, there was a broken window that had aluminum foil up to it. A Cadillac SUV rode by us as we watched the house and then, suddenly, the three-car-garage door rose up. Inside the garage was a bright red Ferrari and a G Wagon. The Cadillac pulled up beside them before the garage closed.

I looked at Murk and he returned my stare before pulling out his gun to check his bullets. I did the same. Mello was definitely in there. It was time to go.

"What we gone do with him?" Murk asked me, nodding his head to Quentin.

I turned around and looked at Quentin who stared right back into my eyes. It was crazy to me how different he seemed now. He was almost normal and looked more like Quan than he'd ever looked since we'd gotten older. Quentin always had a crazed look but, with the medication, the fire in his eyes was gone. That medication did some miraculous shit for that nigga.

"Leave him. He ain't goin' nowhere," I said, still glaring at him. "And if he does, that's one less problem I gotta deal with."

"You sure?" Dame asked and I nodded my head.

"Let's go. We need to make this quick."

Normally, I would have loved to grab Mello and take him back to the warehouse where I could kill him slow, but I didn't even have the energy for that shit right now. What I really wanted to do was put a bullet in his ass and get the fuck out of there. As soon as he was handled, there was nothing standing in the way of me getting Shanecia back.

"Since Quan not here, we all going through the front together," I told my brothers.

"Legend, let me go in with y'all?" Quentin asked, surprising the shit out of me.

"Nigga, what?!" I barked back, turning to look at him. "What make you think I'd let you help me with anything? Nigga, you sit here and count sheep or some shit until I get back!"

Without saying another word, I jumped out the ride and Murk and Dame followed behind me. Within seconds we were in front of the door. With supernatural speed, Murk shot the handle and we charged inside, surprising Mello's ugly ass who was sitting in the living room watching TV.

Mello was kicked back with his arms behind his head and his feet on the table. All of the hate that I felt for that nigga came to the surface as I looked at him. His bitch ass was lounging and shit like he didn't have a care in the world, knowing damn well that I'd murdered his whole damn team looking for his ass. What a bitch.

Once we stormed in, he jumped and instinctively went for his gun that was sitting on the table, but he was too slow. Holding my pistol out, I let off a single shot that went straight through his hand, blowing four fingers straight off.

"FUUUUUUCK!" Mello screamed, his ugly, scarred face contorted in painful agony. His screams were music to my ears.

I lifted my gun to let off another bullet as Murk and Dame stood by my side handling business, but stopped when I heard the front door swing open. I kept my eyes focused on Mello, hoping that whatever the hell was happening, Murk and Dame could handle it.

"Quentin, what da fuck?!" I heard Murk yell out and I let out a sharp curse under my breath.

Without saying a word, Quentin charged up the stairs, running right past us. I turned to Murk and Dame who had bewildered looks on their faces as they both tried to figure out what the fuck was going on.

"That nigga's mind is still fucked up. Follow his ass!" I gritted through my teeth, mad as hell that I'd left him in the back seat tied up instead of in the damn trunk like I'd started to do. You give a muthafucka a chance and they'll mess it up every damn time.

Murk and Dame took off up the stairs and I turned my attention back to Mello, letting off another shot through the arm with his only good hand. He cried out once again and it brought a smile to my face. His ass was sweating bullets because he knew what was coming next. He was living his last moments.

Walking in close to him, I leaned down and glared into his red eyes. Then I wound my hand back and brought my gun forward, smashing the shit out of his mouth, crushing some of his blackened teeth in the process.

"You fuck nigga…you thought you were going to be able to come back and take my shit from me, huh? You thought you could beat Legend, didn't you?" I asked him as blood ran down his lips.

He glared back at me as he breathed out heavy, labored breaths, unable to even say a word because of all the pain. He was trying his hardest not to cry like a little bitch. He wanted to take his final moments like a man. It didn't matter to me how the fuck he took them, he was done.

Pulling my gun up, I placed it right at the side of his head, the tip of the silencer making a deep impression, as I stared at him in the eyes. I wanted the last thing for him to see to be me. That's the image he could carry with him into his next life.

"Any last words, nigga?" I asked him, giving him my signature line.

He clenched his jaw together and sneered at me as blood and sweat ran down his face. I could feel the stench of his fear although he was trying to be brave. He wasn't fooling anyone but himself. He continued to glare at me until I actually thought he wasn't going to try to say anything but then he expelled a jagged breath and his lips began to move.

Peonnnn!

I let off a single shot and the light went out of his eyes as he dropped, the back part of his head flew back on the wall behind him. It was over.

It was finally fuckin' over.

Standing up, I admired my work as an exhilarating feeling came over me. Mello was gone. I'd succeeded and there was nothing stopping me from getting Shanecia back and showing her that I could keep her safe. Her nigga had handled business and that's how it would always be. Wasn't a damn thing she needed to worry about.

Turning around, I ran up the stairs to see what was going on with Murk, Dame, and Quentin. I could hear some thumping and talking but that was it.

"What da hell is goin' on?" I asked as I walked into the room they were in. "We done, time to get out."

My eyes focused on the scene before me and I saw the chick who was riding in the Cadillac dead on the floor next to the bed. It looked like her neck was broken. Quentin was sitting on the bed staring at her with a blank look in his eyes as if he wasn't all there.

"The fuck…?"

I turned to look at Murk and Dame who were standing over a briefcase looking at some papers inside. Both of them had their faces twisted up as they read whatever it was that had caught their interest.

"She was FED," Quentin said, all of a sudden. "When y'all went inside, I saw her through the window taking off her clothes. She had a jacket on that said FBI on the back. That's why I ran up in here to get her before she could get at y'all."

My focus went back to the dead chick lying on the floor with the broken neck. Mello's new bitch was the fucking FBI. This nigga was sleeping with the FEDs. His ass knew how to pick them.

"What's that shit y'all reading?" I asked Murk and Dame.

"He was helpin' her ass…they were workin' together to try to get rid of us. They got all kinds of shit on us but ain't nothing that's gone really stick from what I see. No witnesses and no pics of us really doing shit other than sittin' on the block," Murk told me.

Nodding my head, I pressed my lips together and ran my hand over my face.

"This still ain't good," Dame started. "I know you had to do it, Quentin, but you killed a fuckin' FBI agent. They gone be all over this shit. We gone have to lay low for a bit."

Quentin nodded his head and I looked at him. I wasn't going to give his ass no credit but he did possibly save our life. The chick he'd killed was trained to shoot. If he hadn't gotten to her first, she could have bust a cap in all of our asses before we even got to her. I was so focused on Mello when we walked in, I hadn't even considered that he was messing with someone other than a basic bitch.

"We'll figure all that shit out later," I told Dame. "Call the crew so they can get this shit cleaned up. We can't leave no trace of nothing. Not a muthafuckin' thing. Matter of fact, we might need to go back to how we used to do it and clean this shit ourselves before we light it up. We don't need no witnesses."

Dame and Murk nodded their heads, a grim look crossing both of their faces. We'd been in some fucked up situations before but nothing like this. Never before had we murked a fuckin' federal agent. That shit brought on the kind of heat that we didn't need. Not to mention, it seemed like my connect at the police department seemed to be a little resistant as of late. I was going to have to pay his ass a visit to make sure that he wasn't getting scared and trying to squirm on our special arrangement.

Pushing all of that away from my mind, I started to focus on the task we had before us. There was a lot I needed to consider but my first job was to get rid of these bodies and cover our tracks. Then I could go and get my lady and bring her back where she belonged.

They survive...

Chapter Seventeen

SHANECIA

I looked at myself in the mirror, scrutinizing my appearance for any indication that I was sick, so that it wouldn't be a lie when I told Alani that I couldn't go with her because I wasn't feeling well.

"Don't even try it," she said as she walked up from behind me with her arms folded across her chest. "I already know you're trying to look for an out but there isn't one so don't even. My sister is in there doing the same damn thing but I'm not fucking with y'all tonight. Get it together!"

"Lani, you don't even *go* to Spelman. Why do you care about this mixer?" I asked with my hands up in the air.

"You going. So get your face right so we can get out of here!"

She turned on her heels, making her hair swirl behind her as she stomped out of the where I sat in the bathroom still staring at my reflection.

Tonight, there was a nice little dance that the student union threw in order to celebrate the beginning of the semester. It was also a small mixer so that everyone could get to hang out with each other and make friends or meet other students. When I attended the year before, I loved it. This time, I wasn't feeling it.

Before meeting Legend, these types of events seemed so important but they didn't now. On top of that, I had been messaging Legend all day and he hadn't answered once, so I was feeling some kind of way because of that. Why was he ignoring me?

"My sister is getting on my damn nerves," Trell informed me as she strolled into my room and laid across my bed. "How do you put up with her ass?"

"The same way you do," I replied with a laugh as I applied my makeup. "She won't take no for any answer tonight so I guess we both need to get our mind right."

Trell rolled over on the bed and looked at me. She was really a beautiful woman; even more so than she had been to me the first time I'd seen her. She was broken and hurt then but, most of all, it seemed that her self-esteem suffered some. None of that was apparent now. She exuded a confidence about her that was attractive in a way that caught the attention of everyone around, male or female. Taking a break from Dame and his wild antics in order to get herself together, was exactly what she needed.

"Can I ask you a question?" Trell started as she looked at me while tugging at one of her long braids.

She had her hair styled in long, tiny braids that were loose at the ends and gave way to her wild and curly mane of hair. It reminded me of something Alicia Keys would have done back in the day.

"Yes, you can."

"Do you think Dame has really changed?" she asked with her voice full of hope. She missed him.

"I think that only God knows whether or not he's truly changed but I can't say that I'm not proud of him," I said with honesty. "He has been going out of his way not to repeat his same mistakes. My opinion is that he loves you, Trell. He knows he fucked up and he's sorry. Whether you choose to go back to him or not is your business. This is your life. Don't let anyone tell you what you should or shouldn't do."

After I was done speaking, I could see that Trell had a lot on her mind. She was a woman torn between what her heart was telling her and the murmurings of her mind. I felt for her because I knew exactly what she was going through.

Legend made me weak the same way that Dame did to her. She was an educated woman but, although she could figure out the most complex situations brought about in the classroom, she couldn't understand the deep dark passions of her heart. Love was trivial in a way that we couldn't prepare for. You just had to feel it and push your way through while hoping that you'd come out unscathed and without scars. But Trell had plenty scars inflicted by Dame so I could understand her issue with trusting him once more.

"He's been texting me. I won't answer his calls or reply back to the messages but I turned on my read receipts so he'd know I read them," she told me as she bit her lip. "I miss him, but I just don't want to be stupid again. All my friends…I lost them all behind him. I was the dumb friend that everybody hated to have. The one who goes through shit with her man but doesn't listen to a thing anyone has to say because the next time you see her, she's right back with his no good ass. That was me."

She snickered her disgust at her past actions as I looked on without judgment. I'd been through it with Maliah and, if I'd learned anything in that situation, it was that things were far more complicated than they seemed when it came to the men we gave our heart to.

"Do what makes you happy," I told Trell finally. "Fuck everybody. Do you and let them hate while you're happy."

Shrugging, I started to fix up my hair into a style. I was going to go out tonight and I was going to have fun. This time, I needed to take some of my own advice and just let go and do me. All my life, I thought about what was best for others, but everybody else was now consumed with their own lives and I was miserable.

I missed Legend and I wanted him back so I planned on having the time of my life for this last night because tomorrow, I would be packing up my shit and going back to Miami. I needed a legend in my life.

*****

The party was fun but it wasn't all that popping because it was an academic party, meaning…there was no alcohol. However, the music was good and it was nice to see some of the girls that I'd had classes with the year before. The guys from Morehouse were in attendance and they were *fine*. Sadly, I wasn't interested. I would be getting my man back the next day so I wasn't worried about any of them.

Trell had walked to the bathroom and Alani was hanging with some of her sorors, so I was on my own for the moment, which wouldn't have been too bad…had I had a nice strong drink. Or had Legend been responding to any of my texts.

"Don't I know you?" I heard someone ask. There was a touch on my elbow and I swirled around, coming face-to-face with a handsome face that made me smile instantly.

"Hi…Yeah, I think we had microbiology last year," I remembered as I looked at his perfect white smile. "You play basketball, right?"

He smiled deeply, showing off two perfect dimples in each of his cheeks as he nodded his head. His long, neatly done locs hung to one side in a long, thick braid. He was definitely sexy with broad shoulders and a muscular build. He looked down at me in a way that made me feel minuscule under his large and lean frame.

"Yeah, I play a little. It's just a hobby of mine, really. I didn't see you over the summer."

I shook my head, a pang going through my heart as I thought about my summer with Legend.

"I wasn't here…I went back home to Miami over the summer," I told him.

He leaned into me in a way that wasn't meant to be inappropriate but was definitely flirtatious.

"That's too bad. But I'm glad you're back. It's nice seeing you." He paused and looked me up and down slowly before connecting his eyes with mine. "Wanna sit down somewhere and talk a little?"

Smiling, I was about to agree to a little chat when I felt a change around me. It was like the entire ambiance was altered. There was some shuffling and I saw a few heads turn towards the entrance of the ballroom. Females started to smile and chatter as they looked back and forth between each other and the object of their attention. I moved slightly to the right so I could see what everyone was looking at. But it wasn't *what* it was *who*.

"Oh my God…" I whispered as my stomach did somersaults within me.

At the entrance of the ballroom was Legend and Dame. They were walking in like they owned the place and dressed to a T in what was obviously custom-made designer suits because they fit perfectly. All of the guys in the building were dressed to the nines, but Legend and Dame put each and every one of them to shame.

With Dame by his side dressed simply in an all-black suit, looking straight out of *GQ* magazine, Legend was wearing all white straight down, even white shoes. He had a clean cut and a perfectly lined edge up. His ears were dripping with ice and I caught the sparkles from his diamond-encrusted watch all the way from where I sat. His eyes were searching throughout the ballroom, swooping over the faces of all the people staring at him as he searched for someone. I knew exactly who he was looking for. He was looking for me.

"Legend," I said softly, impossible for him to hear, but his eyes came right to me as if he'd heard what I'd said.

A second later, they swooped over to the man standing next to me and they narrowed in warning.

"You know him?" the guy next to me asked. He shifted his feet and squirmed a bit under Legend's penetrating gaze. He wasn't no punk by any means, but he was still no match for Legend.

Oozing with passion, I nodded my head. "Yes...that's my boyfriend."

"Oh, my bad..." he apologized quickly before stalking away. I barely noticed him leave.

As he made his exit, Legend approached me, his eyes fully on me as he spoke his love into me without words.

"What are you doing here?" I asked in shock and surprise as I looked at him.

I noticed that Dame had already found Trell, catching her right as she walked out of the bathroom. They'd quickly reunited and she was already wrapped up in his arms. Love had won the battle she'd been fighting.

"I came for you," he told me with ease. "I had a little help from Alani."

He smiled in a way that set my heart on fire and made the space between my legs grow hot and wet with pleasure. It was a panty-soaking smile and I never wanted to go another day without seeing it again. As I stared at him lovingly, I noticed something new that made the fire in my heart from him grow into an untamable, savage flame.

"You got a new tattoo..." I couldn't help but grin as I stared at it.

Biting his lip, Legend nodded as he smirked at me. A hummingbird whose beak spelled out my name. It was the sweetest thing I'd ever seen.

"I took care of everything in Miami…you don't have to be afraid to go back. You don't have to be afraid to be mine," he continued, and I felt guilty for what I'd said about him not being able to protect me.

"At the same time, I know that being here is your dream and I don't want to stop you from living your dream. But my dream is to be with you and to always have you in my life. So if you don't fuck with my dream, I won't fuck with yours and we can try this long-distance thing for now. Deal?"

Nodding my head, I wiped away a tear and allowed him to pull me close into a tight hug. He dropped his head and pressed his lips against mine, pulling me into a kiss that I'd waited so long for. In my heart of hearts, I knew that Legend and I wouldn't be apart forever. I was happy to finally have him back.

Chapter Eighteen

MALIAH

"You was talkin' all that shit about workin' because you bored as hell at home, so I got a job for you," Murk said to me. "Get on out the car."

Leaning up, I looked around at our surroundings. We were in front of Legend's house. He didn't have to say a thing; I already could tell Murk was about to be on some bullshit.

"Murk, I ain't gettin' out the car. You bribed me into gettin' in it but I'm not gettin' out because I already know you on one. Why are we in front of Legend's house?" I mouthed off with my arms crossed in front of my chest.

Without answering my question, Murk lifted his hand and pointed to the door handle by my side.

"Out, Li. Or do I have to drag you out like I dragged your ass into this damn car?" he threatened, sending me back down memory lane.

I shifted in my seat as I thought about the way in which he'd gotten me into the car earlier. I knew he was on some crazy shit so

I'd refused to go when he said he was finding something for me to do. Murk wouldn't take no for an answer, so he lifted me up and dangled me over his shoulder. My ass was in the air right by his head.

When I started to kick and scream, he'd eased my thighs apart and started stroking me gently in my most sensitive area. That calmed me down just enough for him to drop my ass in the car as I recovered from an orgasm. His ass was nasty but I loved him like that.

Giving him a sideways look, I thought about whether or not I wanted him to try me like that once again. A smirk rose up on his face as he watched me. He knew exactly what I was thinking.

"Li-Li, get your nasty ass out the damn car. Shit…you a fuckin' freak," Murk laughed as he jumped out.

Sucking my teeth, I rolled my eyes and followed behind him, making sure to slam the door when I got up. Murk scooped behind me and slapped me hard on my ass, making me stumble a little forward.

"Don't be slamming my shit, sexy," he told me with a smile. "C'mon, let's go. You got a job to do."

Five minutes later, I was about ready to kick Murk and Legend's black asses up and down the damn street.

"What the *fuck*?!" I yelled after we walked in a room in the downstairs part of Legend's house.

It was a room all the way to one side, set off from the rest of the house as if it were for a guest. In the room, there was nothing but a bed and a few other pieces of simple, yet tasteful, furniture. But what had my full attention was the fact that Alicia's ass was tied up in the damn bed, sweating and murmuring incoherent words under her breath.

The bed was soaked beneath her and her hair was plastered to her head and drenched with sweat. Her mouth was moving a mile a minute and her eyes were closed. I wasn't even sure she knew we were in there. But, worst of all was the *stench* in the room.

Alicia smelled like nothing less than old ass farts with a side of shit. When I say that she was so rank, I mean…she was so smelly that my nose tried to run the fuck straight off my damn face. Turning, I looked at Murk but he seemed unbothered by the entire scene as he stood next to me with his normal stoic expression on his face.

"This is your work," he informed me with ease. "Legend's been trying to get her clean. She's going through withdrawals. Since he's been gone, I've been coming over here to take care of her. But since you're so bored all the time…"

He looked at me with a smile on his face and I swear I wanted to slap him so hard that the imprint of my diamond would be left on his forehead.

"Bullshit," I replied back. "Get da fuck out of here…she needs a doctor!"

"Legend has a nurse that stops by from time-to-time to check on her and take her vitals so she don't die." He said that last part so detachedly, like he couldn't care less one way or another. "You just need to wipe her down and feed her. Shit like that. I wouldn't untie her, because she's little but she'll beat your ass so she can rob you and get out of here to score something."

"Isn't this…illegal?" I asked him quietly as I looked at Alicia's thin, frail body, tied, and bounded by the rope at her wrists and around her ankles.

Turning, Murk gave me a completely bewildered expression with bug eyes and his mouth parted slightly. Just then it dawned on me how stupid my question was. What the hell did Murk and Legend care about something being illegal? Every damn thing they did was illegal! Thankfully, he cleared his throat and continued on, totally ignoring my question.

"I'll be back to pick you up later before the kids get back from school. Have fun."

He smiled and swatted me on my ass but I returned his stare with a horrified one of my own. I know he was not about to leave me with Alicia. What the hell did I know about getting someone clean? And, honestly, I never liked her ass and definitely didn't like her after seeing that she'd slept with Danny!

"Don't leave—"

"Aye, she's your fam," Murk told me. I gave him a sideways look to let him know that I did not consider Alicia fam worth caring for so he adjusted his approach.

"She's Neesy's mom. Legend is trying to get her clean and he just needs our help until he gets back or until she's well enough to put into a program."

Sighing, I slumped my shoulders in defeat and turned back towards Alicia as Murk walked away. She was still dripping sweat and mumbling to herself. I felt overwhelmed just looking at her. Where the hell do I start?

"Well, first, I'm going to give your nasty ass a bath," I said, pinching my nose as I glared at her. "And second, I'm calling my damn mama so she can help me with this shit."

*****

"Girl, what in the world you tryin' to get me into?" my mama shouted as soon as she walked into the guest room and saw Alicia on the bed.

She'd finally fallen asleep about ten minutes before my mama had arrived but with as loud as she was, she was about to wake Alicia right back up. I'd gotten her to fall asleep by releasing one of her hands from the ropes after I'd wiped her down and helped her to drink. After that, she was out like a light. Unfortunately, her mattress was still soaked in only God knew what, so the smell still remained.

"Shhhhh!" I hushed her with my finger to my lips. "I don't want you to wake her up. Then she'll start moving and blowing that shitty smell around."

My nose twisted up as I looked at Alicia. I hadn't fully untied her yet and, from the smell of it, the mattress underneath her was soaked with feces and urine. I don't know what the fuck Legend was thinking but his ass should have been here to deal with her. I couldn't wait to get home so I could kick Murk's ass for doing this to me.

"Ah, hell naw," my mama cursed, shaking her head before pinching her nose. "Her ass smells like a sewer even while she knocked the hell out. She can't get no damn worse than that. Bye, Maliah. I'm outta this bitch."

I gawked at her with my eyes wide open as she tossed me the deuces and started towards the door.

"Mama! You can't say that! You're supposed to be a good Christian," I countered.

"Fuck that and fuck her," she continued to my amazement. "The damn smell coming from her done ruined my religion. You know I never liked that hoe anyways—"

"Do it for Neesy, Mama," I said, using the same trick Murk had tried on me. "You know it destroys her to see her mama like this. Please?"

Slowly, my mama turned around with a scowl on her face and a look in her eyes that told me she knew that I was baiting her but she also couldn't turn me down. Of all the people in the world, Shanecia was the one person who always gave of herself to others. She was the most selfless of us all and, if ever she needed a favor, our family would pull together to get it done.

"Well, I ain't touching *that*," my mama said with her upper lip turned up in disgust. "So let's go down to the Dollar Tree and get a bucket, some soap, some long ass surgical gloves, scrubs, masks, hair nets...hell, I need a damn suit them scientist used on that movie with the monkeys spreading the killer disease if I gotta mess with her disgusting ass."

Gasping, I looked at my mama and shook my head slowly as I spoke though clenched teeth.

"Mama, damn! Can you at least watch what you sayin'? She's not dead...she can still hear!"

"She can't hear shit," my mama shot back quickly. Sensing my dismay at how she was acting, she pushed past me and walked over to where Alicia was and clapped loud, inches from her face.

"See? She is dead to the world!" she said as she turned around to face me.

Suddenly, Alicia's eyes jumped open, scaring the shit out of me. She reared up and grabbed my mama around the wrist with her one free hand and I screamed loudly from shock.

"Loretta, help me, pleaaaaaase!" Alicia wailed loudly with her voice cracking in a way that seemed painful.

"OH MY GOD! SOMEBODY KILL IT!" my mama screamed as she jumped damn near three feet in the air.

Alicia had a death grip on her wrist and still didn't let go. Before I could run over to help her get loose, my mama grabbed her purse in her free hand and started pelting it hard against the top of Alicia's head over and over again.

"KILL THE BEAST! GOOD LORD ALMIGHTY---SOMEBODY HELP!" she continued to yell as she beat the shit out of Alicia's head. "NAW, BITCH. LET. GO!"

"MAMA!" I yelled out as I rushed to her and snatched the purse out of her hand.

Alicia looked slightly dazed and confused, but otherwise fine. Reaching out, I pried her hand off my mama's wrist and she quickly moved away to the other side of the room, as far away from Alicia as she possibly could.

"Mama, why you hit her like that?!" I asked as I used a napkin to push the little scraggly pieces of Alicia's hair off of her face. "She ain't do nothing to you to deserve that!"

"What the hell you mean?!" she said while breathing heavily and holding her hand to her chest. "I nearly died! Sweet Jesus, wrench the stench up off of me!"

Rolling my eyes at her disrespectful and dramatic ass, I turned back to Alicia who was sitting quietly in the bed beside me. When she saw my eyes on her, she lifted her head up and whispered in a small voice.

"I just wanted some mo' water."

Her lips made a dry, smacking sound as she spoke. Pursing my lips, I reached out for the jug of water that Legend had next to her bed and helped her drink from it. Once she was done, I sat it down and looked at her.

"We're going to take care of you today. We will be right back, okay?"

She nodded her head and tried her best to give me what looked like a smile. From the looks of it, the worst of her withdrawal process was pretty much over. She seemed lucid enough but I wasn't taking any chances. Her ass was going to stay tied up until I got back.

Turning around, I looked at my mama who was leaning on the wall with her arms crossed and an ugly frown on her face, as she looked at Alicia who wasn't even paying her the least bit of attention.

"Mama, let's go," I told her as I rolled my eyes.

Should've left her ass right at home.

"You would think that you would be cool with this being that you used to be a CNA!" I fumed as I walked out of the room.

She sucked her teeth as she trailed behind me.

"Yes, girl, but I treated *humans*. I haven't the slightest idea what that creature is in there. I'mma need to get my Bible before I come back in here."

Chapter Nineteen

LEGEND

"**N**igga, when you comin' home? I got Li tending to Boogie, but that ain't gone last long. She gone kick my ass when I pick her up from over there," Murk said through the phone.

I laughed thinking about how he'd told me that he just up and left his chick in my crib to care for Shanecia's mama. That was some funny shit but it was exactly something I'd expect from his ass. She'd been telling that nigga she was bored and needed something to do. Well, she got exactly what she'd asked for because one thing Boogie was not was boring. Her ass was a muthafuckin' handful but I knew that the worst of it all should pass soon. The withdrawal period wouldn't last too much longer.

"I'll be back soon...I'm checkin' out the city right now," I told him as I cruised through a part of Atlanta I was told was called East Point. "They got some interesting niggas out on the block out here. Amateurs."

Shanecia had left for class and I decided that I wanted to explore the city. Alani had been staying with some friends while I was there, but I still didn't feel comfortable just sitting in a house all day. Plus, Shanecia's apartment was filled with a bunch of girly shit. What the hell I looked like just sitting up in her shit with my feet kicked up? Naw, that fruity shit wasn't for me.

"Cruising round the city, huh?" Murk asked me in a way that let me know he knew what was on my mind. "Nigga, it sounds like you out plottin' to me. Don't fuck around and don't come back."

"You know my heart bleed 305, nigga," I told him with a light chuckle.

"Yeah, but it used to bleed 954. And before that it was bleeding something else. I know how you move, Legend. Don't forget, I been by your side every time you set your eyes on a city you wanted to take over," he reminded me.

"You ain't never lied, nigga. Aye, let me hit you back." My eyes had just fell on some niggas who looked about as official as it seemed like I was gonna get at the moment. They still looked like petty hustlers but I knew they would be able to help me out with what I needed.

"A'ight, nigga," Murk told me before he hung up.

I placed the phone in my lap and then rolled up real slow next to two niggas who were chilling on the top of a dingy stone wall. While I'd been watching them, I saw a chick who was an obvious fiend walk up to one of them and get her fix for the night. The nigga who had handled her seemed to be the youngest of the two, but he took out a knot of cash from his pocket after she'd paid him.

"Aye," I called to the youngest one.

He gave me a suspicious look but I was ready for it. He was a street dude and he ain't know me from any other nigga. I could've been coming to rob him or set his ass up. He ain't know.

Cautiously, he walked over moving his hand to his side where I knew he had his piece stashed.

"What's up, nigga, I know you?" he asked as he looked at me with one side of his lip curled up.

"Naw," I told him as I looked back at him square in the face. He tittered a bit when he saw that his intimidation methods weren't working on me but I saw him relax a bit. A street nigga knew another street nigga so one thing he knew for sure was that I definitely wasn't the police.

"Well, what you want then?" he asked me with one brow lifted.

With my head, I nudged towards the fiend who was happily walking down the street in the opposite direction.

"I'm lookin' for some work," I told him.

Silence passed between us as he continued to scrutinize me, staring daggers straight into my eyes. I returned his gaze, refusing to back down. I didn't do that shit. I didn't back down for no nigga whether I was in my city or not. The dude's eyes flickered towards his friend who was still standing to the other side of us.

"What kind of work you talkin' 'bout, nigga?" he asked as he looked me up and down. He moved closer and I saw his eyes sweep through the inside of my car.

"Nothing but the best."

"Nigga, you ain't tryin' to work down here, is ya?" he asked, his eyes trailing back up to his friend who was watching with his hand in his pocket, caressing his banger, I was sure. I had to play this shit right because I knew that some niggas in the hood would see my ass as an easy lick and try to rob me without giving me shit.

"Hell naw. This ain't my city. I'm from Miami," I told him. "Just up here tryin' to buy some shit to take back home."

"Miami?" the friend on the wall piped up, all of a sudden interested in our conversation. "Aye, I used to live in Miami. Matter of fact, you look familiar. What you say yo' name was?"

I ain't say what my name was, I thought to myself.

"Legend."

Immediately, the goofy looking ass dude on the wall's back straightened up and his eyes grew wide.

"Y—you are Legend?" he asked in a way that almost made me laugh. He said my name like I was a celebrity or some shit. I was used to it in Miami but I wasn't even in my city so the shit was hilarious to me.

"Yeah, ya heard of me?" I asked him and he nodded his head.

Reflexively, my hand inched closer to my waist where I had my piece stashed. These days when somebody said they knew me, I honestly didn't know if they were friend or foe so I had to be ready.

"Aye, man, what you want?" the dude continued. "Whatever you want, we got it for the low."

"Nigga, is you buggin'?" the man next to me said through his teeth. He glanced at me before cutting his eyes back at his friend.

"You know you fuckin' up, right?" he asked through his teeth in a way that let me know that his ass had been planning to rob me. I'd already figured that and I was ready to bust first if he tried it. I wasn't new to this shit.

I should fuck your ass up with a hot one to the dome just for thinkin' that shit, my nigga, I thought to myself. *But I'll save that for when I got my niggas with me.*

"Hell naw, I ain't fuckin' up," his friend said. "This is *Legend*, leader of the *D-Boys* out of Miami. The Dumas brothers. Trust me, nigga, give him whatever the fuck he askin' for."

He gave his friend a look to let him know that he was serious and then turned to me.

"Aye, man…Legend, I heard that Rick Ross shouted you out in a song. You and that nigga cool?" he asked me.

I laughed and scratched at my jaw. "Word? Yeah I fuck with that nigga a lil' bit. He was the C.O. when one of my niggas got locked up and he looked out a lil' bit. Now what about that work? I got some shit to do. How much can I get for five?"

The guy next to my window bug-eyed as he looked at me, making me think he'd never gotten that much money at one time. I had to hold my laughter back. These small time niggas would be perfect for my new team.

"Pull off for a minute so we can talk business. I can get you whatever you need. G-shit, my nigga," he said, holding his hand out for dap. I reached out and bumped my fist with his.

"I'm Rodney, by the way. They call me Rod. And that nigga over there, his name is Travis but I like to call him Fat Nigga Trav," Rod laughed as he pointed to Travis.

"Rod, fuck you, nigga! Legend, man, don't listen to shit that nigga got to say. He don't know how to fuckin' act in front of company. You can call me Trav," Trav informed me, cutting his eyes at Rod who was still laughing.

I shook my head at the two of them, thinking immediately about Quan and Dame's dumb asses. I needed to check on my niggas to see what they were up to. I hadn't heard from either one in a while. I knew Dame was probably wearing Trell's ass out, but Quan wasn't up to shit and I hadn't talked to him since before I left for Atlanta. Making a mental note to holla at him as soon as I was done, I got ready to get out of the car to discuss business.

*****

I nodded my head at Rod and Trav as I drove away and dialed Quan's number. The day had been productive and I hadn't even had to waste too much time. The product that Rod and Trav had was good but it ain't have shit on mine. From the way they looked at the bread I'd spent with them, I could tell that they weren't use to making no real money and with me, I could promise they would.

Atlanta was mine for the taking. I just had to play my cards right.

"What up, fam?" Quan's voice said over the loud speaker in my car.

"Aye, nigga, what you been up to? Ain't heard from yo' ass in a minute."

"Awwww," Quan said in a playful tone. "Don't tell me yo' mean ass is missin' a nigga?"

"Hell naw," I said with a light chuckle as I caressed my goatee. "Just wanted to make sure you handled our little problem and wasn't on some bullshit. I know how you get when it come to that fuck nigga. Always wanna save his ass and shit. You can't save everybody, nigga."

Quan didn't respond right away and I frowned as I bent the corner.

"You there?"

He sighed before speaking. "Yeah, I did what I needed to do. It's handled, bruh."

"Aye, Quan, I know you got a bond with Quentin that can't nobody understand," I started. "I was reading some shit in one of these books Neesy got and it was talkin' 'bout twins and shit…'bout how identical twins are split from the same eggs and sometimes when one is cut the other can feel it—"

"Nigga, do me a favor and stop readin' that college shit," Quan laughed as spoke. "This educated shit don't even sound right comin' out yo' mouth, nigga."

"Anyways, I know that you wanna save his ass but it's best this way."

"But he helped you get at Mello, Legend! You wouldn't have gotten his ass had it not been for Quentin. Don't that count for somethin'?" he asked me.

"Hell yeah," I told him as I pulled in front of Shanecia's apartment.

She had the blinds open and I could see her watching TV in the living room while wearing some sexy ass dress. I was gonna fuck her ass up when I walked in there. The hell she thought she was doing giving all these dumb ass college niggas who lived 'round here their own private peep show?

"I gave that nigga the only pardon he deserved when I saw he was still in my city but didn't drop his ass. Quentin ain't right, Quan. He can only blame his fuck up daddy for some of the shit he did, but he can't blame him for all of it. He had a choice and he made the wrong one. Fuck that nigga for life."

"A'ight, Legend. I gotchu, nigga. When you comin' back?" he asked right when I jumped out the car.

"I'on know yet," I told him honestly as I sat on the hood of the car and lit a blunt, still watching Shanecia through her blinds. "But I'll pull through when I get there. Holla at you later, nigga."

I hung up the phone and placed it in my pocket. When I looked up, I saw a young nigga walking up, his whole head turned so he could look inside Shanecia's spot.

"Muhfucka, what da hell yo' stupid ass lookin' at?!" I shouted at him, shocking him to the point that he nearly jumped five feet in the air.

I laughed to myself as he scrambled away. Placing the blunt to my lips, I took a long pull and let it out slow as I thought about the new takeover I was planning.

Atlanta was about to be my new city.

Chapter Twenty

TANECIA

There wasn't a damn thing that Darin could say to convince me that his baby mama didn't still want to fuck. I didn't care what he told me, I knew it to be true. First of all, his ass was sexy. Second of all, *once again*, what woman *doesn't* want to be with her baby daddy after first finding out she's pregnant? And third, the heffa wouldn't stop calling his ass and it was getting on my damn nerves!

"That was Jenta again?" I asked in a confrontational way.

I was heated. It seemed like her ass had a radar on his dick or something because every damn time I was getting ready to try his ass, here she goes calling his damn phone. It was getting frustrating to say the least. I understood that she was a first time mother, but did she have to call him about *everything*?

"What you mean by 'again', Tan? The last time she called was three days ago!" he asked with a frown as he tucked his phone in his jean pocket.

Unnecessary details, I thought of his wonderful reminder.

Reaching out, I grabbed my glass of water off the counter and started sipping to make myself feel less childish about how I was acting.

"And anyways, I asked her to call this time. I wanted to ask her to dinner."

The water went right down the wrong pipe and I immediately started choking. Dropping the glass, I grabbed at my neck as I damn near coughed up a lung and tried to focus enough to tell myself that I had not heard what I thought.

"What you mean you invited her for dinner?" I asked him with my hand to my chest as soon as I was able to catch my breath.

Can you believe the whole time I was choking that Darin's ass didn't make one move to come over and save me? He simply stood, straight-faced, with his arms crossed at his chest as he watched me almost die. I was starting to have second thoughts about his ass.

"Tanecia, I invited her to dinner, that's what I mean. You are my lady and she's going to be the mother of my child. You don't think you two should at least meet?" he asked me with wide eyes.

"Nope!" I said, sending my own set of wide eyes right back at him. "Why would I want to break bread with the woman who wants my man?"

Darin gave me a look that said, had he been a lesser man who put his hands on women, he probably would have slapped me clear out of my damn chair.

"Jenta doesn't want me, Tan! I keep telling you that! What the hell is your problem with her anyways?"

Pursing my lips, I cut my eyes at him and started scrutinizing my manicure. I was not in the mood to be answering his crazy ass questions. If he didn't understand women by now, it wasn't my damn role to be explaining it to him.

"I'm about to cook and you *will* be in here and you *will* meet her. I'm not playin' this game with you, Tan. I'm getting enough heat on me from her father as it is. The least you could do is try to be supportive!" he fumed back at me.

He had some nerve talking about someone being supportive. Not once had he tried to see shit from my perspective. I was expected to be the girlfriend who just sat by and happily watched her man tend to another woman's beck and call without saying a word while no one thought about my feelings in all this shit.

"Fine," I told him as I stormed off towards the bedroom. "I'll do it for you, but I hope you don't expect me to be nice and shit because that ain't happening!"

Slamming the door behind me, I ran into the bathroom to run a bath so I could calm down. This was going to be a long damn day.

*****

"She's here," Darin announced after checking his phone.

He'd undoubtedly received a text from Sweet Jenta announcing her arrival. She probably wanted him to meet her at the curb, scoop her out of the car, and help her into the house. Or maybe lay down on the damn ground so she could walk to the door on his back.

"Yeah okay, whatever," I grumbled as I rolled my eyes.

"Baby, can you please just *try* to be nice," he asked me as he stood up to walk to the door. "This is awkward for all of us but I need this. I don't ask you for much…damn. Give me a little help, bay!"

Swallowing the lump in my throat, I rolled my eyes one more time and then nodded my head. He was right about one thing…Darin never asked me for shit. But he'd been the main one to step in and take care of me after I'd gotten shot, so I could try to set my issues to the side for a night if that's what he needed.

"Hi Darin," I heard Jenta greet him as soon as he answered the door and I fought the urge to roll my eyes yet again.

Standing up, I smoothed out my already curled to perfection weave and walked over to the front. Everything about my appearance was on point because I'd be damned if Jenta came over showing me up in my own shit. Well, Darin's shit but it was where I lived anyways.

My makeup was on point, I was wearing a beautiful Prada dress that probably cost more than Jenta's old ass Dodge truck, and I had on some expensive Balenciaga slides that I hadn't worn in ages but were just right for the occasion.

Darin walked back inside with Jenta right beside him, and smiled when he saw me already standing at the entrance of the dining room waiting.

"This is Tanecia, or Tan. Tan, this is Jenta," he introduced with a broad smile.

With a large, refreshing grin on her face, Jenta pushed her hand out towards me.

"It's so nice to meet you, Tan…although I feel like I know you already. Since we met, Darin has always talked so much about you," she gushed.

Oh you mean while you and him were fuckin' each other? I thought to myself. *Girl, get the fuck out of here with this nice act. You aren't foolin' anyone.*

With my lips pressed together into a forced smile, I shook her hand quickly before letting it go. An awkward silence hung in the air between us, so I shot my eyes at Darin who seemed mortified as he stared back at me.

"What?" I asked him with a shrug.

Instead of answering me, he cleared his throat and turned to Jenta.

"Um, you two can go ahead and sit down in the dining room. The food is done so I'll bring it in. You know what you want to drink? We have water, soda, juice…"

"I'll just take some water," she said in a happy tone that made me sick to my stomach. "Let me start with that and then I'll get to the hard stuff later…maybe have a sip of Coke or something."

Her and Darin laughed at her lame ass joke and I rolled my eyes. The more I looked at her, I just couldn't stand her. She was pretty…I supposed, in an earthy, Erykah Badu kind of way. Her clothes looked like they came from the flea market down on Sunrise Boulevard, her hair was coarse and pinned up in a natural style that I guess was fashionable…somewhere.

But despite her obvious low-maintenance, flea market swag, she was confident and radiated an aura that instantly showed me why

189

Darin had been attracted to her initially. He said that whatever they had was casual but now I was definitely doubting it was. She didn't seem like the type of woman whom anyone had a casual fling with. God, I hated her.

We both sat down as Darin went to get Jenta's water and the food. I made a mental note that he hadn't even bothered to ask me what I wanted to drink. This whole thing was bullshit.

"I don't want him," Jenta said suddenly, as soon as Darin was out of ear-range. "We're having a baby, but I'm not interested in Darin. We're just friends who will raise a child together. You seem uncomfortable with me and I just thought you should know that."

Crinkling up my nose, I looked at her and saw that she had a calm expression on her face as she spoke calmly. She seemed like she wasn't trying to be confrontational but I took it that way anyways.

"And if you did want him, do you think you could make him get rid of me?" I shot back.

Frowning with confusion, Jenta shook her head gently and tried to explain.

"No, I didn't mean that at all…I was just saying that—"

"Well, thank you, Jenta, for not wanting my man so that I can have him to myself. I appreciate that," I snarled as I rolled my eyes and looked off to the side.

There was dead air between us as we listened to Darin preparing our meal in the kitchen. Sighing, I rolled my eyes again and prayed that the night would pass quickly.

"I just want to get along. It's good for the baby and it's good for Darin—"

"You don't have to tell me what is good for my man," I snapped back. "I'm perfectly capable of figuring that out on my own!"

"Tan," Jenta started with nervous laughter as she looked at me incredulously. "Why are you so angry inside? What have I done to you? You look at me with hatred but…how could you? I've done nothing to you. All of this is a product of something that happened before you came into the picture. I'm sorry that it happened that way but I mean you no harm."

She reached out to touch my hand, but I snatched away and glared at her. I was sick of her already. She was trying to play the 'perfect angel' card and make me out to be the villain just so she could go and cry to Darin later and play the victim. I knew the kind of woman she was because I'd been her.

Before I got with Mello, I pretended to just be a friend that he could depend on to talk to when things went left with his wife. Playing the role of a confidant when he was mad at her led to us being only a skip and a jump from fucking. After I got him to trust me and see me as someone who only wanted to be there when he needed me, he started to want me to be there in other ways too. Jenta wasn't fooling me.

"Stop with that bullshit act, Jenta!" I spat at her with my eyes narrowed on her face. "You come in here with your Lauryn Hill vibes and shit, talking about peace and laying your little passive aggressive threats down to make me think you don't really want Darin, but I see through that shit and I'm not fooled. What woman wants to have a baby by a nigga and not try to be with him? I saw you crying and shit when you came to tell him you were pregnant! Don't try to act like this is the ideal situation because it's not!"

"TAN!" Darin yelled as he walked into the dining room holding the pan of food in his hands.

His eyes were wide in shock but the more he looked at me, they begin to narrow in fury. Finally, he placed the food down on the table and turned to me. Grabbing me up by my arm, he pulled me out of the dining room and didn't stop pulling until we were in our bedroom. Closing the door behind us, he pressed his hand to his forehead and expelled a long sigh before he turned back to me.

"How could you say that to her?" he asked as he glared at me. "Do you really feel those things? You've never even met her!"

"I don't have to meet her to know how she feels, Darin!" I yelled as tears came to my eyes. "Or did you forget that I was once pregnant, too? As much as I knew that Mello wasn't the one for me, I still wanted it to work with him for the sake of our child. You can't tell me she doesn't feel the same way!"

Walking over, Darin grabbed me tightly by both of my shoulders and looked me square in my eyes.

"Tan, she doesn't feel the same way! We were never like that! I respect her for the woman she is but that's not what our relationship was about!" Darin explained.

He released me and a few tears fell down my face. I was so upset but it had to be deeper than me being angry about Jenta and Darin because that shit wasn't worth crying about.

"You never properly mourned the baby," Darin said quietly as he watched me carefully. "That's what this is about."

"What?" I asked him as I wiped away more tears. Why the HELL couldn't I stop crying?!

"The baby…the one you lost," he continued. "You never properly mourned and this situation is awakening that anger in you."

I shook my head as I sat down on the bed and turned away from him. This had nothing to do with my baby and everything to do with him and his baby mama who was trying her hardest to come between what we were building. Why couldn't he see that?

"You can't be mad at Jenta, Tan. You have to get through what you're going through and mourn for what you've lost, but you can't take your pain out on someone else," he said to me in a quiet voice.

Walking over to me, Darin kissed me on my cheek and walked away. I clenched my teeth down hard, but the tears continued to pour down my face, further frustrating me because I couldn't get them to stop. I didn't know what was wrong with me, but I felt like it was a little fucked up that Darin wanted to blame it on the child that I'd lost. This had nothing to do with my baby. This was all about him.

It's all about him and that bitch, I thought to myself as I drifted off to sleep. *This is about him.*

But even as my eyes grew heavy, I knew deep down that Darin was a little right. I missed my baby and I wanted what I'd lost to be given back to me. As I started to go to sleep, I couldn't ignore the light sound of laughter as Darin and Jenta continued on with the dinner without me. They were talking and laughing with ease and comfort…

like a happy couple.

I was losing everything I'd ever wanted and Jenta was popping in and getting it all.

Chapter Twenty-One

MALIAH

"SHIT!" I cursed as I dropped to my knees, straight down to the bathroom floor. "Fuck…fuck…fuck!"

I was devastated.

Just when it seemed like everything was going according to the plan that I'd set for myself, God threw a monkey wrench right in the middle of it all and pushed me off course.

Well, if I were honest with myself I had to say that I couldn't blame this one on God. I knew full well what the hell I'd been doing to get to where I was. Or…I knew what I *hadn't* been doing was more like it. And what I *hadn't* been doing was taking birth control and what Murk *hadn't* been doing was wrapping up.

So now, here I was, sitting on the fucking bathroom floor with three positive pregnancy tests on the floor with me. That morning, I'd realized that two months had passed and I hadn't had a period. I was so caught up in taking care of Alicia and the kids that I didn't even realize I was missing it.

"FUCK!" I cursed again when I opened my eyes and saw all three of those damn plus signs.

"Aye!" Murk's voice surprised me on the other side of the door. "What's goin' on in there? You havin' problems takin' a shit?"

Scoffing, I rolled my eyes at him. This was the man I chose to be my baby daddy.

"No, Murk!" I shouted back at him. "Go away! When the hell you got home?!"

"Da fuck you ask me that for, Li! I live here! When da fuck did you get home, nigga?" he barked back.

I could tell he was joking but I was not in the mood. My mind was too focused on the fact that I was pregnant by a man whose main punchline of every joke was the fact that I had 'twelve damn kids' or how 'fertile' I was. On more than one occasion, Murk talked about how we had enough lil 'nigglets' running around. And here I was pregnant with another one. This conversation wasn't one I was ready to have.

"Aye, open up this damn door! What you doin' in there if you ain't shittin'?" he grumbled as he started turning the doorknob. Too bad it was locked.

"MURK, GO AWAY!" I yelled as I started cleaning up the pregnancy tests. Once they were all in my hand, my eyes began darting around for a place that I could hide them where Murk wouldn't look.

My tampon box! I thought as I reached over the counter to grab it.

Just as I had it in my hands and began stuffing the tests inside, I heard the door unlock and Murk pushed it right open.

"The fuck you doin' in here?!" he asked with his eyebrows crinkled in confusion as he eyed me suspiciously.

"Murk!" I yelled as I tucked the box behind my back. "How the hell did you get in here?"

Stopping, he looked at me like I lost my mind.

"Whatchu mean?! I got a key," he replied easily as if everyone had a key to their bathroom doors. "What the hell is that behind your back? What you hidin'?"

Backing away, I tried to move away but, before I could, he reached behind me with his long ass arm and snatched the box right out of my fingers. Not even bothering to first look inside, he walked over to the sink and turned it upside down, dumping all of the contents. The three pregnancy tests made a clanging sound as they fell into the sink at the exact moment that my heart dropped to my feet.

Watching him intently for a trace of a reaction, my breathing stalled when he did nothing. Murk didn't move a muscle or even flinch as his eyes looked down into the sink at the tests, each with the result side up and a big ass plus sign staring back at him. My throat got tight as I waited for him to say a word.

Then suddenly he turned towards me. On his eyes was an awkward expression and his eyes were wide. Reaching up, he scratched at the top of his head in a bewildered way and his pupils rolled to the ceiling as he thought hard about something before he focused back on me.

"So um…" he started as he scratched at his jaw. "You pregnant?"

Pressing my lips firmly together, I nodded my head slowly.

"That's what the tests say."

"Is it mine?"

My mouth dropped open. Grabbing the toilet paper, I threw it right at his head. It hit him smack on the forehead even though he'd tried to duck out the way.

"The hell you mean?! Of course, it's yours!" I shouted. "I should have known you would say some stupid shit like that Murk! If you don't want to have the baby, we don't have to have the baby! But I'm not going to have you insulting me like I'm some hoe or some shit. I told you I didn't sleep with Danny and I didn't!"

Tears came to my eyes but I blinked them away as Murk just stared at me, allowing me to vent before he started to speak.

"Get dressed, Li," he said after I'd calmed down some. "I'mma take you to the doctor so we can see how far along you are."

Clenching my teeth, I simply nodded my head and walked to get my dressed and put some shoes on. I would save my yelling for later after he received proof that my baby was, in fact, his.

"And chill, a'ight?" he told me as he came up behind me and tapped me lightly on my shoulder. "I know the kid is mine. That was just some dumb shit that came out my mouth because I didn't know what the fuck to say at first."

Nodding my head, I turned him around and looked him in his eyes.

"I meant what I said though. If you don't want the baby, we don't have to keep it."

Murk backed away and pulled his hand from me as if I'd offended him.

"Have I ever gave you a fuckin' reason to think I wasn't a real nigga?" he asked me.

My eyes shot wide as I tried to think of what in the world I'd said to make him react in that way. Shaking my head, I thought over my words carefully as I spoke them.

"N—no, why would you think—"

"A man takes care of his responsibilities, Maliah. I knew what the fuck I was doing when I nutted in you all them times! Shit, I'd have to be stupid not to! You already got a bunch of damn kids!" he explained angrily with his hands out.

See what I mean? His ass was always talking shit about the amount of kids I had. I hated his ass.

"That's my jit in there, just like the other three are. If I let you get rid of that one, we kicking Dej, Jari, and Sha's lil' asses out too because obviously you with a fuck nigga who don't give a damn," he finished as he looked at me with his piercing hazel eyes and I swooned.

Ghetto love. That's what we had.

It had to be because he was borderline cussing me out and reading me to the fucking *filth*, but all I was doing was getting wetter and wetter. He was sexy as hell to me in that moment.

"Now get your shit together so we can go see 'bout my seed," he commanded and I hopped to it.

"Yes, daddy," I told him with a smirk.

A smirk teased his lips as he watched me and I knew that all was well between us. For now, anyways.

*****

"WHAT THE FUCK YOU MEAN?" Murk cursed as he gawked at the doctor like she had four heads instead of one.

Sighing, I pressed my fingers to my forehead as the doctor gaped right back at Murk, obviously confused by his behavior. She'd said something that she'd expected would excite him and here he was... acting like a nigga.

Sitting back in his chair, he crossed his arms in front of his chest and gave her a pointed look as he tilted his head towards the monitor beside me.

"Look at that and run this by me one more time," he asked her in a cool tone.

Dr. Caviar, whose mouth was partially open and whose face was tinged pink with embarrassment, cleared her throat and then looked back at the screen. Lifting her hand, she pointed as she spoke.

"This is one head...you see it here, right?" she paused and waited for Murk to reply. When he didn't, she continued.

"And *this*...well, this is the other baby's head. So you have twins—"

"Twin what?" Murk asked. He was in shock and any old crazy thing was just popping out of his mouth. For a savage street king who had seen and experienced many things, he was not at all prepared for this and it was obvious.

"Twin *babies*," she clarified, looking at me for help. I just shrugged at her. Welcome to my life. There wasn't a damn thing I could do with his ass.

"It's too early to tell the sexes of the two just yet but I can tell you that, if everything goes well, you're going to have two babies in about... seven months."

"How the hell I come in here to see about one and end up with two of these niggas?!" Turning, he looked at me like I was an alien. "Oh baby making ass...I knew this shit was too good to be true."

Sighing, I couldn't help but roll my eyes at his dramatics. The resident doctor in the corner, a young Black girl who seemed to be in her mid-twenties, was having a kick out of the entire thing as she looked on. She had to turn away in order to hide the fact that she was trying her hardest not to laugh.

Dr. Caviar looked back and forth between me and Murk as she tried to gauge our reaction in order to decide what she should say next. We weren't giving her nothing at all to go off of. To be honest, I was excited about the prospect of having twins. Although when I'd initially found out I was pregnant, I'd been upset about it, thinking about having two of Murk's bighead ass babies at one time had me elated.

"I need to smoke a blunt," Murk said and pulled it right out of his pocket just like he didn't have no gotdamn manners. Dr. Caviar eyes bugged so far out of their sockets, I thought they would fall onto the floor. The resident doctor, unable to hold her laughter any longer, burst out so loudly in hilarious chuckles that she had to exit the room.

"OKAY! *Don't* light that until you leave...and definitely not around her," Dr. Caviar requested as she stood up. "I'm going to give you all some time to decide what you want to do. I'll be back in a minute."

"Oh we know what we wanna do, Doc," Murk said right as she started to leave. "We ain't gettin' rid of my seeds but after you pull them two out, I'mma need you to lay them to the side so you can tie her shit up so we don't have no more."

Dr. Caviar gasped and looked at me for a response. Once again, I shrugged. She cut her eyes back to Murk before walking out of the room. As soon as she was gone, I let my head fall into my hand before lifting up and looking at Murk.

"I swear, I can't take you no fuckin' where, Pablo," I muttered as I glared at him.

Without saying a word, he stood up and walked to the bathroom with the blunt situated nicely between his fingers and his lighter in his other hand. I rolled my eyes and laid back down flat on the bed. I already knew what he was up to.

"Just two puffs to get my mind right and then we can go," he announced before closing the door behind him.

I really didn't know how I was going to put up with his ass.

*****

"I'll be back, okay?" Murk told me as he pulled into the driveway.

Nodding, I didn't say anything as I unlocked the door and got out. The entire way home, he'd had a million thoughts on his mind...I could tell just by looking at him. But he didn't say a thing to me. I trusted him but I couldn't say that I wasn't feeling a little put off by how he was acting.

As soon as he found out we were having twins instead of only one baby, his entire attitude had changed. He'd been beating his chest and shit earlier talking about how he was a man who handled his responsibilities, but he sure seemed like he was singing to a different tune now.

"Mommy! You're back!" Shadaej squealed as I walked in the house.

Seconds later, Dejarion and LeDejah were right behind her. Each of them ran up to me and wrapped their little arms around me, pulling me into a tight hug. After planting kisses on each of their foreheads, I walked into the living room where my mama was so I could deliver the news. But before I could say a word, she stood up and handed me a letter.

"I have my mail being forwarded here. This letter is for you," she told me, giving me a look that told me whatever it was had to be about Danny.

As soon as I looked down at the letter, I knew it definitely was. Although he hadn't left a name and only a return address on the envelope, I knew Danny's handwriting anywhere. The kids ran down the hallway, laughing and playing, and I sat down on the couch as I ripped the envelope open.

Maliah,

I'm still trying to get clean. I...I don't want to tell you what happened but a few months ago, I woke up and I was in a place I knew damn well I shouldn't have been. Drugs make you do some fucked up things and I think I've finally learned my lesson. I can't even begin to tell you what I've done…

I paused from reading, knowing that he had to be talking about sleeping with Alicia. There was no coming back from that shit. I knew his ass had to be traumatized.

…When I'm clean, I'll do as you asked. I'll stay away but I still want to be able to see my kids. We can do it your way but I want to see my kids. Please tell them I love them.

Danny.

After reading the letter, I folded it and placed it back in the envelope. I didn't even have to look up to know that my mama's eyes were on me, scrutinizing my every move.

"You good, baby?" she asked me with a tenderness in her voice that was exactly what I needed.

Nodding my head, I bit my lip. Tears came but I kept them away. For anyone who has ever had to get over their first love, it's not an easy process. No matter how much I thought I'd moved on, every now and then I'd realize that a small piece of me hadn't. It wasn't enough to get me to leave Murk, but it was enough to make me wish for the best for Danny and hope he would be okay. No matter what, I wanted him to be happy just as I was. I still wasn't even over the fact that Murk had tried to hurt him, but I couldn't admit that to him. Murk would never understand the emotional connection I had with Danny. But, honestly, it was probably the same one he had for me. Even if we weren't together, I was sure he wouldn't want anyone to harm me.

"I'm good, Mama," I told her, honestly. "I just wish things were different, you know?"

She nodded in a way that let me know she understood exactly what I was trying to say.

"You can't want someone's happiness more than they want it, Maliah Michelle," she told me wisely. "When he wants it bad for *himself*, then he will get his life together. Don't worry about him. Us Black women *worry* over our Black men way too much…we handicap them with our fears. We hold our sons close when we should let them be free…experience life and learn how to be a man." She paused before pressing her lips together as tears came to her own eyes.

"That's what I did with your brother," she admitted tearfully. "I held him much too close when I should have been pushing him out and letting him learn how to be a man…how to be responsible… how to *earn* things instead of being given everything or taking it from others. Now he's in prison because I shielded him away from lessons he needed to learn."

Standing up, I walked over to her and hugged her as the tears fell down her cheeks. I never knew that she blamed herself for Talon being in prison serving a life sentence.

"What Talon is going through is not your fault, mama!" I told her as I wiped her tears away. "We are grown and we make our own mistakes. You loved us…you raised us on our own and you taught us right. The fucked up things that we go through are *not* because of you!"

And I meant every word. In the past I'd been guilty of trying to blame my mama for some of the things that had happened to me but, truth was, it wasn't her fault at all. She'd raised me right and I made my own decisions.

"Mama, I have to tell you something," I told her finally as I sat down in the chair across from her.

She'd stopped crying but her eyes were still wet and puffy. Sniffling a bit, she looked at me with expectant eyes and waited.

"Murk and I went to the doctor today..." I started, filling a joyous feeling creep up in my chest. "...and I'm pregnant. With twins."

"WHAT?!" she yelled, pressing the palms of her hands against her cheeks. "Are you for real?!"

Nodding my head, I couldn't help the smile that came across my face.

"Well, where is Murk?" she asked, instantly dimming my smile. Sensing something was wrong, she frowned.

"He—he dropped me off and left," I divulged with a somber tone. "He was excited at first...and then he found out there were two instead of one. I don't know what he's thinking now."

"I don't know what he's thinking either...leaving my baby here alone like this," she scoffed as she rolled her eyes. "But what I do know is that Murk is a man and you have nothing to worry about. One thing about him is that he wasn't shielded from *shit*. I can guarantee you that wasn't no damn body worried about his crazy ass when he was growing up so, unlike Danny and Talon, he learned all his lessons about being a man," she added emphatically, instantly making me smile.

It was no secret that Murk had a rough upbringing. Although he kept much of it secret, I did appreciate what he'd gone through because it made him an incredible man today.

Before I could say another word, the door to the garage opened and Murk walked through it. He had a blank, unreadable expression on his face that I'd long ago gotten used to seeing, as he stomped in, totally forgetting to take off his dirty ass Timberlands.

He tilted his head slightly as a greeting to my mother and she replied back with a quick and curt 'Hey baby'. From there, his hazel eyes bore into mine like an infrared beam as the stoic expression on his face kept intact, blocking me from even guessing at his thoughts.

Walking over to where I was, he stood in front of me, looking down on my face. I wanted to speak but I was caught up in a trance as I stared back up at him. I didn't know what to say and couldn't speak if I could. Then, in the next second, he took my breath away.

Dropping down to one knee, Murk pulled out his right hand that I hadn't even noticed had been tucked in his pocket. In his hand was a black box that he held out in the palm of his hand as he kept his eyes focused on me.

Twisting up my lips, I glared at the box, not wanting to get my hopes up too soon. Behind him, my mama had her hand to her heart and tears were in her eyes. If she knew like I knew, she would be waiting for a minute before she got excited too.

"This better not be no empty box, Murk!" I yelled as I grabbed it from his open hand.

His face stayed serious as a heart attack. He didn't even start to crack a smile. And that's how I knew this had to be the real deal.

I opened the box hurriedly, not wanting to torture myself a single second longer. There, right smack in the middle, sat the most beautiful ring I'd ever seen. It was a pink diamond, in the shape of a teardrop. I got one good, short glimpse of it before tears clouded my vision.

"Maliah, I know I'm not good enough for you," Murk started in a voice so soft and gentle it almost didn't seem like it belonged to him. "I know I'm a fucked up man and I have a lot of issues. I don't always do shit right and I don't always say the right things…"

Through my tears, I snorted out a laugh. He was right for damn sure. He barely *ever* said the right things.

"…But I love you more than I love myself. And I love our family more than I love myself. I'd die in a heartbeat for any person in the house right now. If you'll take me, I promise my life to you for the rest of my days. I know I was trippin' earlier…but I wanna raise our little village you've created for us all together. God knows yo' baby makin' ass doin' all you can to nail a nigga down for life."

Snorting again, I rolled my eyes. A proposal from Murk wouldn't be right if he didn't take a jab at me in the process.

"So…will you marry me?"

"YES!" I yelled as I nodded my head and wrapped my arms around his neck. Standing up, he lifted me in the air before planting on my lips the most passionate kiss he'd ever given me. The kiss, his touch, the way he held me…all of it felt different to me and, hell, it should! I was officially wifey now and would be the wife soon! I had the ring and all and Murk would soon be officially mine.

What we had wasn't a fairytale but it was a real tale of true love and I couldn't see my life without him.

Chapter Twenty-Two

SHANECIA

Hanging up the phone, I took a deep breath and let it out slowly as I ran my hands back and forth down my thighs, another nervous habit that I'd developed recently. I'd just finished speaking to Maliah and, although I was happy about her news, I couldn't say that I wasn't somewhat put off by the fact that Legend hadn't mentioned marriage once to me.

Any time anyone brought up the subject, he either acted like he didn't hear them or changed the topic to something completely different. And now here Maliah was…she'd called me squealing on the phone about how she was not only expecting to have twins with Murk, but was also engaged to marry him. And I had been with Legend longer!

"What the hell you got that sourpuss look on your face for?" Legend asked me as he strode into the room with his phone in his hand.

I watched him as he strode in. My thug of a man in all of his sexiness but, as always, dressed simply in shorts and a tank while lounging at home. His attention went back and forth between me and his phone as he pecked out a message but waited for my reply.

"I don't have a sourpuss face, Legend," I said in a pressed tone, which all but proved his assumption that I was in an ugly ass mood.

Legend's stare focused on my face for a few minutes as he scrutinized me once more before returning to his phone. After pushing a few more keys, he dropped the phone in his pocket.

"This ain't got shit to do with your cousin, do it?" he asked me with a raised brow.

I bit my lip and wondered if I should say anything about what I was really thinking. I'd always been taught that you couldn't rush a man when it came to marriage because it never worked out in your favor. But, at the same time, hell, he asked!

"Well, I—"

"Because we already talked about this shit…you in school. We can't be makin' no damn babies," Legend reasoned, cutting me off as he stood in front of me with his arms crossed in front of his chest.

"Babies?" I repeated with a frown.

Of all things going on with Maliah and Murk, namely an *engagement*, he thought I was jealous because she was pregnant with twins.

"I don't want no babies right now, Legend. That's not what I was—"

"Well, what the hell you over here looking at me with that stank ass face for?" he countered, his eyes boring into mine.

Blinking, I felt myself getting aggravated but swallowed hard and tried to calm myself down before I slapped him dead on his face.

"I'm not looking at you crazy because of the babies, I just—"

"You know what, I don't got time for this shit," Legend interrupted me one last time as he turned to walk away. "One day you want babies and the next day you having a fuckin' fit because I nutted in you and you wanna wait until you graduate and shit. Make up yo' muhfuckin' mind."

The source of my aggravation quickly disappeared down the hallway and I let out a long, tight exhale of frustration. When he wanted to be, Legend was really an asshole. An asshole who I loved more than life, but an asshole still.

"Grrrr!" I growled as I snatched one of the pillows behind me and squeezed it tightly between my hands, wishing like hell that it was his face.

"Listen, Hulk Hogan…when your crazy ass stop strangling pillows and shit, put some shoes on. I wanna take you somewhere," Legend's voice rang in, shocking the hell out of me. I hadn't even heard him walk back in the room.

"You wanna take me where?" I asked him, dropping the pillow to my side. "I don't feel like going anywhere with you right now."

"See, I didn't ask you all that, Neesy! That mouth is the reason why I ain't 'bout to put no babies in your ass right now," Legend pointed out as he ran his finger along the hair on his chin in a way that drew my attention even in my anger. "Get your ass up and let's go."

Shaking my head, I frowned as I stood up to walk down the hall to put on some clothes. When I passed by him, I scowled right in his face but he smirked back at me instead.

"I don't know why you got an attitude because a nigga won't drop a baby in you," he taunted as I walked down the hall away from him. "You act like a baby every damn day. I can't take too many more of that shit."

LEGEND

I had the biggest damn surprise for Shanecia, but leave it to Murk's dumb ass to ruin the shit for me. Right when I get ready to show her what I did to secure our future together, I walk down the hall and hear her on the phone with Maliah talking about how she had just tricked Murk's ass into asking her to marry him. Well, 'tricked' isn't the words she'd used but that's what I called it because I knew damn well my damn brother wasn't the marrying type. She had to have tricked that nigga. Either way, I knew better than to walk into that conversation so I turned around and jogged right back into the bedroom and hit his love drunk ass up.

Nigga, you asked ole girl to marry you???

Seconds later, he responded with the bullshit.

Yeah, nigga, she pregnant. With TWINS! I knew her breeding ass was gone get me for some jits. But I love her so Ima make it official.

"*Hell* naw!" I spat as I dropped the phone down on the bed beside me and waited until Shanecia finished talking.

This was some bullshit for real. Any time a chick heard that her girl was getting married, the next thing she started thinking was that her ass needed to be next. And that wasn't where my mind was right now. I wanted to be with Shanecia but I couldn't say I was ready to marry her just yet.

For one thing, she didn't listen to *shit*. What nigga want a wife who does what the fuck she wanna do all the time? Secondly, I still wasn't convinced she really wanted to commit to what it took to be with a nigga like me. And last, and most importantly, once I let a chick lock me down, I was locked the *fuck* down. I only had one marriage in me so that shit better work.

I loved the hell out of her but if I was married to her when she tried to run like she did a few months back, I would have snatched her up and chained her ass to a door handle or some shit. I mean, I would've went straight Samuel L. Jackson from *Black Snake Moan* on her ass in this bitch. Once I decided a chick was going to be my wife, she was just that: *mine*. There was no turning back. Ever.

"You still ain't tell me where the hell we goin," Shanecia fumed from beside me.

Once again, I played dumb and acted like I didn't know why she was so pissed off.

"Stop bein' so damn impatient. You act like you ain't got no damn manners sometimes. Shit!"

She snapped her neck at me so fast that I was surprised her head didn't roll right the hell off.

"You should talk! You ain't never had no damn manners!"

I didn't even respond to her statement. Even if I wanted, I couldn't because I was cracking the fuck up inside. She was more upset than I'd ever seen her and, at this point, it wasn't even just because of the fact Maliah was engaged and she wasn't. It was because she wanted me to know why she was mad and I wouldn't give her a chance to tell me. She was frustrated and pissed off to the max, but I was getting a kick out of that shit.

"You know what?" she started. "Just drop me off on the corner and I'll catch a ride back. I'm sick of you."

"You ain't going no damn where, Neesy. We're all the way in Alpharetta. Have you even been this far?" I asked her, already knowing the answer.

Without responding, she laid back on the seat and continued to pout to herself. She was a big ass baby.

I give you about five minutes, I thought as I made a turn which brought us closer to our destination.

Biting my lip to try to squash my pending grin, I peeked over at her and saw that she was squinting as she stared out the window trying to figure out where we were going. I made another turn and we were situated in front of a grand, gated entrance. There was a letter on each door of the gate. Pure gold Ds. Easing up to the keypad, I pressed in a code and the gates opened.

I peeked over at Shanecia once again and saw that her face completely changed as we drove down the winding road that led to where I was taking her. She was in awe as she took in the scenery of a large, plush lawn covered with rose bushes and many other exotic flowers. But it was when we pulled into the tremendous, circular driveway that she gasped and covered her mouth with her hands.

Done, I thought to myself as I checked my watch. *In three minutes instead of five.*

"Welcome to your new home," I told her with a smile as I put the car in park.

"WHAT, LEGEND?!" she squealed as she jumped out of the car

and looked at the beautiful mansion I'd just closed a deal on. "You're lying!"

She ran up to the door and I followed slowly behind her, slowing down to nearly a snail's pace on purpose just to annoy the shit out of her.

"Hurry up and open the door, damn!" she yelled, stomping one foot with her hand on her hip.

I laughed to myself and then walked up, taking my time to find the right key and put it in the lock, while she stood beside me huffing and puffing. Once the door opened, she shot inside and I promise, Shanecia touched every damn wall inside of the house as she explored each room yelling and screaming about how gorgeous it was. And it was nice. I'd been fortunate enough to be able to buy it with the furniture that they'd decorated it with because neither me nor Shanecia knew shit about decorating and we damn sure didn't have the patience.

"You like it?" I asked her once she was done exploring.

"I *love* it," she corrected me as she planted three soft kisses on my lips.

"Well, it's yours," I told her. "Well, ours…I'm staying in Atlanta with you."

Shanecia's eyes grew wide and her mouth dropped open even wider.

"You're what?! How are you going to do that? What about—"

I placed my hands up to stop her. The last thing she needed to be worried about was money or what I did in the streets. The less she was involved and the less she knew, the better. Murk was right. I couldn't involve her in what was going on with me. She wasn't built for that shit. She was a good girl.

"All you need to know is that I'm stayin'," I said. "I'm stayin' with you and this is yours. In your name…just in case you decide you wanna kick a nigga out."

Sliding her arms around my neck, she pulled me close and kissed me on my lips.

"I'll never kick you out," she told me. "I love you."

"I love you too."

Chapter Twenty-Three

TANECIA

The sound of Darin's phone ringing in the dead of night instantly put me in a bad mood. I knew exactly who it was and, even though I'd had a talk with Darin about her plenty times before, the fact that she was calling once again at such an ungodly time of the morning still bothered me.

"Hello?" Darin grumbled in a raspy tone when he answered the phone.

I rolled over on my side and squeezed my eyes tightly shut, hoping that would drown out the sound of Jenta's frantic voice on the other end. She probably wanted nothing important at all. Probably was calling Darin just because her back was hurting or she wanted some Cheetos or some shit. This whole situation just annoyed me and I still didn't really understand why but it just did!

"What?!" Darin yelled out all of a sudden as he jumped out of the bed. "What do you mean you're going into labor? Jenta...you're only seven months along!"

Now that woke me up. I sat up on the bed and watched as he started putting on his clothes, unsure of how I should react. Should I get up and help him? Should I go with him? What the hell was a woman supposed to do when her man's baby mama was about to have their baby? Did this kind of shit happen often enough that I could Google an answer?

"FUCK!" Darin cursed after he'd hung up the phone.

I looked at him and saw that he had tears in his eyes which made a lump form in my throat. All of a sudden, all of my selfishness melted to the side. Something was terribly wrong and he was scared. I could see it all over his face.

"I have to go," he told me in a pressed tone as if he were trying to keep it together. "Jenta's at the hospital. She didn't want to call me to tell me that she was having contractions because she thought it was false labor and she was trying to be conscious of how you feel about her calling…"

The way he said that made me feel like shit. His tone almost felt like he was blaming me for something. Swallowing hard, I ducked my head down to look at my fingernails and continued to listen.

"…Anyways, she's in labor and she's going to have the baby but she said there are complications…Shit! She's only a little over seven months, Tan! The baby may not survive!" Darin said as he looked at me.

His eyes were wet and it was obvious that he was under a huge amount of stress. Whatever issues I had going on in my mind about the fact that my man was having a baby with another woman needed to be squashed. This was happening and it was about to happen now. But what Darin needed was for me to be there for him. I had to sit myself aside and focus on him. I couldn't be selfish…which was what I was used to being so this was definitely going to be some work.

"I—I'm going to go with you," I found myself saying as I slid out from under the covers.

"No, baby, you don't have to—"

"I want to," I said as I interrupted him. "We are going to all have to make this work together so we can start now. Plus, you're in no condition to drive. I got you, baby."

The relief in Darin's eyes showed through instantly and I knew he was gracious that I had put myself to the side and thought about what he needed. It was necessary…I knew what it was like to be expecting a baby and to be afraid that the child wasn't going to make it. In the moments after I'd been shot, that's exactly how I felt. I thought I was going to die but what was most terrifying to me was the fact that my baby would not survive. It was the worst feeling I'd ever felt and I knew exactly what Darin was going through. I couldn't let him go through it alone.

"Okay, I'm ready," I told him after I'd pulled on some shorts and stuffed my feet in some shoes. I wrapped myself up in a sweater to cover up my nightshirt and grabbed the keys to the car. There was no time to get glammed up. This was an emergency.

A family emergency.

*****

When they let us back to see Jenta, I looked at her and instantly my heart started bleeding for her. She looked exhausted and scared. Her skin was pale and her lips were dry. She was covered in sweat and her hair was soaked to her face. Her parents, who I had met briefly while in the waiting room, were next to her, each holding one of her hands as she experienced each contraction that seemed to take a piece of her with it whenever it went away.

When her parents saw Darin and I walk inside, they looked at us and I saw they both looked about as bad as she did. Her mother, a very attractive, regal beauty with the smoothest ebony brown skin, was crying silently as she watched her daughter go through absolute turmoil. Jenta's father's face showed his strength and also his devastation. He wasn't crying but his eyes were rimmed in red as he helplessly watched his daughter wince in pain.

"We'll give you some time alone. Frank, can you go with me to get a drink?" the mother said as she turned to her husband.

Frank shot her a look that made it obvious he wasn't in agreement to be anywhere other than by his daughter's side but, he stood up anyways. Leaning over, he kissed Jenta on her forehead and then walked over to his wife and grabbed her hand.

"Let's hurry and go so we can come back, Tracey," he told her as she placed her hand in his.

As they walked by us, Tracey gave Darin a tight smile but Frank wouldn't even look at him. It was obvious that Darin was not his favorite person at all. Looking at Darin with a sympathetic expression on my face, once again I felt guilty for not being there for him more than I had in the past few months when it came to Jenta. It was starting to become obvious to me that he'd been going through a lot that he hadn't shared with me. I could tell Frank had probably been giving him and Jenta hell about their situation.

"I—I'm sorry about da—daddy, Darin," Jenta said as she winced through what I figured was another contraction. "You know how he is about this."

She tried to chuckle but it came out dry and painful instead of how she'd intended it. Walking to her side, I took the place of her father and sat down next to her, grabbing her hand. She shot me a soft, gracious smile, letting me know that she was happy for the embrace and it warmed my heart. I squeezed her hand tighter as I returned her smile.

"What's goin' on, Jenta? Why aren't they giving you something for the pain?" Darin asked.

"Th—they can't," she told him, tears coming to her eyes. "I'm too far along and they don't want to numb me because I won't be able to push."

"Did they say why the baby is coming early?" he asked and she shook her head.

"No...but it's your child, Darin. So I guess it does its own thing just like its daddy." She shot him a pressed smile and then grimaced as another contraction passed through. I felt my heart sting when I heard her comment, but the way that she squeezed the shit out of my hand instantly made me forget all about it.

"I'm sorry," she apologized and gave me a genuine look after the contraction had died down.

"Don't mention it," I said although I really wanted to cuss.

Then her eyes began to do a weird thing where they rolled back in her head and I felt my heart leap in panic.

"Jenta?!" I yelled, jumping up out of my seat.

"Huh?" she mumbled as she blinked and tried to focus on me but she couldn't. Her eyes were dancing around in her head. She was exhausted. Something was wrong.

"Fuck this shit," Darin said. "I'm going to get the doctor."

And with that, he stormed out of the door, leaving her and I alone. Jenta began to moan and she released my hand to begin running both of hers over her belly.

"Are you okay?" I asked her. She nodded her head but she didn't look okay at all.

Standing up, I walked over to grab a rag and I wet it with cold water. When I went back over to her, I ran it over her forehead, cleaning the sweat off of her face but also cooling her in the process.

"Thank you," she said in a soft voice.

I nodded and continued to run the cloth over her head, hoping that it made her feel better.

"Listen, Tan, I know that it's been hard for you," she started. "I'm sorry for that but I understand. Who wants to start a relationship with someone and find out that he has a baby on the way?"

She laughed a little at her comment and I joined in with nervous laughter as I removed the cloth and sat back down by her side.

"I've never wanted to mess up what you two have. I've never

wanted to come between that. What you two have is beautiful. Darin needed someone to love and I'm glad he has you." She smiled and grabbed my hand in hers. A shadow passed in front of her eyes and she looked away before bringing her attention back to me.

"I—If something doesn't go right with me...please, just know that I couldn't have chosen a better woman to help Darin raise our baby. I really do admire you...from everything that he's told me about you since I met him, I know that you are a wonderful woman and you have great strength...even if you haven't realized it yet."

Tears were streaming down my eyes and I didn't even know it until she reached out and wiped one away.

"I'm so sorry for how I've acted with you," I told her, finally as I continued to cry. "I didn't know why I was so angry but now I know exactly why. A little before you showed up, I'd lost my own child...it wasn't Darin's but it was loved and wanted. When I saw you and Darin told me that you were expecting his baby, I hated you for it because I was jealous that you were getting something that I wanted so bad...and with the man who I should have always been with. So, you see, I didn't dislike you at all...I disliked myself for how I'd fucked up my own life being with men who didn't want me when the only man who I should have been with...the only one who had ever loved me...was right here. I'm so sorry I was so damn evil! I just couldn't think about your baby without being angry about mine."

Jenta shook her head softly from side-to-side as she reached up and wiped away another one of my tears. She flinched as she experienced another contraction and then waited for the pain to subside before she continued to speak.

"Everything we go through is to prepare us for where we are supposed to be. Just believe that. Nothing is done by accident. Every situation is designed to make us into the people God wants us to—"

Suddenly, her eyes rolled back in her head once more and she released her grip on my hand. The monitor next to her that had been beeping rhythmically started shrieking in alarm, a long, sharp droning sound emanated from it as I began to panic.

"JENTA!" I screamed, jumping up just as her body went limp. "JENTA!"

Reaching over her, I pressed down hard on the emergency button and waited for someone to pick up the line.

"Please come now! Something is wrong with her! PLEASE!" I screamed.

Just then, Darin, followed by Jenta's parents, rushed in. I moved back as they pushed by me, each of them grabbed at Jenta, shaking her as they tried to get her to respond.

"What happened?!" Darin shouted as he looked at her with tears in his eyes. "JENTA!"

Tracey began to howl as she stared at her daughter with her hands to her mouth. Frank was murmuring incoherently as he grabbed at his daughter's hand, trying to wake her.

With my hands to my mouth, I started to cry as I backed away, unable to take any more of the tragic scene around me. Turning around, I ran out the door just as the emergency staff rushed in. Out in the hall,

I sent a prayer up to God that He would save her. In only a few minutes, she'd become a close friend of mine and I needed her to survive.

God, please.

*****

At 4:46 a.m. in the morning, Darin's daughter was born, weighing in at only 4 pounds, 3 ounces. At 5:10 a.m., after holding her daughter and kissing her for the first time, Jenta was pronounced dead.

My heart ached in my chest when I got the news as I sat in the waiting room. I was all cried out and couldn't even bear to shed another tear.

"Do you want to see her?"

I looked up and my eyes fell on Tracey standing above me, her eyes puffy and red as she looked down at me. Nodding my head, I stood up and grabbed the hand that she'd held out for me.

"We have to be strong," she told me as we walked down the hall. "For Jenta's sake." Her voice cracked when she said her daughter's name. "You know, she only had good things to say about you. I'm happy that you're part of my family now."

Tracey looked at me and I smiled sadly as we walked into the NICU ward. Standing in front of the glass, I looked at the rows of newborn babies, some sleeping and some awake…all various sizes, weights and colors. All precious. Tears came to my eyes once more as I'd thought about my angel baby.

"She's over there…at the end of the third row," Tracey told me.

I looked and when my eyes fell on her, I immediately smiled. She was beautiful with dark brown skin just like her mother, and a head full of the curliest jet black hair I'd ever seen. She was incredibly alert for a premature delivery and looked extremely healthy.

"She's beautiful," I whispered. I was in awe of her.

Tracey smiled and stared at her granddaughter. We sat there in silence for a while, looking. Then suddenly, the baby started to stare off into the distance above her and a wide smile crossed her face. She started to giggle and coo as she looked at something only she could see. If I hadn't seen it with my own eyes, I swear I wouldn't have believed it.

Holding my hand to my chest, I gasped and when I looked at Tracey, tears were streaming down her face.

"It's Jenta," she said through her tears. "My Jenta is playing with her baby girl."

Chapter Twenty-Four

LEGEND

A week later...

I looked at Murk and he nodded as he stared back at me. Turning to Dame, I saw he was all up in his damn phone with a sick ass grin on his face.

"Nigga, what you doin'?" I asked him, with my lip curled up.

"Sextin' with Trell. Let's hurry this shit up so I can get back up in them guts," Dame said as he slid the phone back in his pocket.

"Yo' ass just left, Trell. Da hell y'all sexting for?" Murk laughed as we all got out of the car.

"Man, you go as long as I did without having no damn pussy and you'll find out," Dame argued his point. It was a valid one too. I would be happy as hell if Shanecia would send my ass a naked pic or two every now and then.

"Hell naw," Murk shot back as we walked to the door. "I ain't tryin' to do that shit."

"What? Go without pussy or sexting?"

"Both!" Murk quipped as Dame laughed.

I knocked on the door and then stood back with my hands clasped behind my back. Murk cleared his throat and scratched at his jaw as he waited, and I tried to stop the thoughts from circling in my mind of how I was going to beat Quan's ass if I walked in this bitch and saw Quentin sitting in the living room farting and shit on my damn couch.

Although Quan claimed that Quentin was gone, I wasn't convinced because he still was actin' so fuckin' *weird*. He hadn't been to the rec center with us in a while before I left, and every time anybody called him, he seemed too busy to actually be on the phone. On top of that, nobody had really hung out with this nigga in months. Something wasn't right.

The lock turned in the door and seconds later, Quan opened up the door, but only enough for him to look out.

"What's up? What y'all doin' here?" he asked as he peered back out at us.

Tilting my head, I squinted at the nervous expression on his face. He looked like he was about to shit his pants. He was standing in front of us with his shirt off, showing off his bare chest, and a pair of basketball shorts. It looked like he hadn't shaved in a minute, too.

"The fuck up with you, nigga?" I asked him. "You can't let us in? What you hidin' up in there?"

"I ain't hidin' shit," he lied. It was an obvious lie.

Before he could say anything else, Murk and I pressed through the door, knocking his ass to the side. I pulled my gun out and held it to my side. If Quentin was in here, I wasn't going to kill him but I damn sure would pistol whip the fuck out of his ass. I'd never admit it but I was grateful that he'd helped me grab up Mello and killed that agent bitch, but his ass still was going to get fucked up for still being in my gotdamn city.

"Y'all...wait!" Quan called out. "What y'all doin'? Quentin ain't in here!"

"Well, we gone see for ourselves," Murk said as he and Dame walked in behind me. "So pipe down, nigga."

Dame grabbed Quan by the arms before he could get in front of us and stop us, as we headed down the hall. I heard some movement coming from the back and I knew exactly who it was. Quan had fucked up majorly by going against what he'd said he would do, and as soon as I punished Quentin's ass, his was next.

Pushing the door open, I stormed in with my strap out.

"MUTHAFUCKA, WHAT DA HELL YOU STILL DOIN' HER—"

My mouth clamped shut when I saw it wasn't Quentin in the room at all. It was a chick. A pretty ass, half naked big girl.

"Agh!" she screamed as she shot her hands up in the air and jumped backwards onto the bed.

"Oh shit!" Murk yelled as he came in beside me and looked at her.

She was a large, very voluptuous and curvy female, lying on the bed wearing a skimpy maid outfit. She was pretty as hell and scared shitless.

"Nigga, put down yo' fuckin' gun!" Quan yelled out, struggling against Dame's tight hold.

Dame released him and he stepped forward and pushed my gun down as the three of us sat stunned, our eyes pinned on the female in his bed.

She was definitely a BBW…a big, beautiful woman. Not at all the type that I'd pegged for Quan's skinny ass. He was muscular and had a nice, athletic build like a basketball star but what the fuck could that puny nigga do with a chick like that?

"This nigga done scooped him a *grown* muthafuckin' woman," Dame joked as we watched Quan lovingly tend to his chick to make sure she was good. "All this time we thought he was up to some bullshit and his love-sick ass been over here fuckin' a thickums!"

"Can y'all get the fuck out of here?!" Quan snapped, looking at us as we watched him comfort his woman.

Not paying attention to shit he said, we all stayed put, in awe at the fact that he'd finally looked like he was settling down with someone. Not the playboy who split plates and shit with chicks…hell, naw, not Quan. I couldn't believe my nigga was actually in love.

"I ain't goin' nowhere. All y'all niggas done seen what my fiancée's working with so fuck all y'all," Murk said with a chuckle. "Damn, I can't believe this shit!"

We watched as Quan handed the woman a glass of water to calm her down. She drank it all down quickly, trying her hardest not to look at the three of us. Walking over to the bed where the woman was sitting, Murk held his hand out to her using his most proper voice.

"Aye, ma'am, my name is Murk. I'm Quantinarion's brother." He turned back towards us. "That's Legend and Dame and we're all pleased to meet you. Now who are you and how long you been chillin' with our brother, Quan?"

Quan frowned and pushed Murk away. "Nigga, get the fuck out of here. All y'all get out of here!"

Laughing, we all walked out of the room. Quan came out last and closed the door behind us. Then he walked down the hall to the other room and peeked inside before closing it behind him.

I narrowed my eyes at him and followed him down the hall.

"Who the hell in there?" I asked, pointing at the door.

"You got *another* chick in there too?" Dame asked. "The fuck kinda organization you running up in here?"

"A hoe house," Murk piped up as if he was certain what he said was fact. "My nigga, if that's what it is, I want in. Them shits be makin' more money than the dope game—"

"Muthafuckas, get y'all asses the fuck down the hall," Quan grumbled. "I ain't runnin' no fuckin' hoe house!"

We all walked back into the living room and sat down quietly, all of our eyes on Quan as we waited for him to explain what the fuck was going on.

"So…my nigga, is that yo' chick we saw in there or your bottom bitch?" Murk asked, breaking the silence.

Quan cut his eyes at him and scratched at his jaw like he wanted to slap the shit out of him.

"Nigga, that's my lady! I been chillin' with her for a minute, but I didn't want to tell y'all niggas because you think everything so fuckin' funny and…well, you know, she…"

"A big gul," Murk clarified for him with a shrug.

"Naw, she juicy," Dame said with a smirk on his face. "Mo' cushion for the muthafuckin' pushing! That's what the hell I'm talkin' 'bout, nigga. Give me some dap, nigga!"

"See what the fuck I mean?" Quan said with an exasperated sigh as he shot his eyes at me. I tried to keep the smile down on my face but, truth was, I was cracking up on the inside about the whole thing. It was about time Quan get a dose of his own medicine.

"I hate y'all niggas," Quan scowled.

"You can't act like that, Quan," I told him. "Yo' ass always teasin' everybody and now you wanna catch feelings 'bout this little shit? Ole crybaby ass nigga."

Murk was staring at the ceiling, running his finger along his mustache slowly as if contemplating something, and then finally lowered his gaze to Quan.

"So…I just wanna know, is it true what they say? Like…can you fold her up like a pretzel when you givin' her the dick?" he asked. "Maliah thick and shit but I can't fold her up like that."

"Hell yeah, that shit is true," Dame answered for him. "You remembered that thick booty ass Brazilian chick I was with back in the day? Best pussy I ever had…other than Trell, of course. I could fold her up in ways I ain't *never* been able to do a skinny chick! Them bones could bend but damn sho' ain't break."

Crossing his arms in front of his chest, Quan fumed in silence as he cut his eyes back and forth between our brothers while they took turns teasing him. He wasn't enjoying himself but it was what his ass got. Quan always teased us about every damn thing. It was about time his ass got some of it.

Why he thought we gave a fuck about his chick's weight, I had no idea. Hell, who fuckin' cared how much a woman weighed? If she did it for you, was loyal, took the dick right, and had something in her head worth having, wife her ass up and show her to the world. If she was yours, let everybody know that shit.

"Y'all niggas done or what?" Quan asked as Murk and Dame collapsed in laughter at his expense.

"Yeah, we good," Dame asked, wiping at his eyes as he continued to laugh.

"Nigga, is you cryin'?! It wasn't that fuckin' funny!" Murk laughed, punching him on the shoulder.

"Hell yeah it was," Dame continued to chuckle as he wiped at his eyes some more and then pointed at Quan. "You see that nigga's face? He over there in his feelings!"

Watching them, I shook my head and let out a little laughter before something came to me.

"Who is that in the other room then?" I asked Quan.

"Her daughters. They stayed the night over here," he replied, still pouting with his mouth poked out.

"Wait!" Murk said with his eyes up like he remembered something. "This wouldn't *possibly* be the chick you tried to split the plate with? The chick you said with the nappy head ass daughters who caught an attitude because you wouldn't pay the sitter?"

We all looked at Quan and his light toffee-colored face flushed slightly red, letting us know that Murk was right.

"AW, HELL NAW!" the three of us said as we started cracking up laughing.

"All jokes aside," Murk finally said after our laughter died down. "Why you been hiding her from us?"

With his eyes wide, Quan stared at us incredulously as if to ask 'you really don't know'?

"Look how y'all actin'! I didn't say nothing because I knew y'all would tease me about the shit! But listen, I don't care how big she is! I love her and that's it. And fuck whoever got shit to say about it," Quan spat with his chest up like he was threatening us to say something about his chick.

"Quan, stop that stupid ass shit, nigga," Dame said, waving his hand at him. "Don't nobody give a shit about how much your chick weighs. It don't matter what female you call yourself being in love with, we was gone clown your ass because you always ridin' on us about every damn thing. Your jokin' ass can tell a joke but you can't take one, huh?"

A sheepish look crossed Quan's face as he realized that he was getting mad over nothing. He'd only been getting a taste of his own medicine. A little payback for years of what he'd done to all of us.

"Don't hide your chick," I told him as I stood up. "If you love her, flaunt that shit. Don't make her feel like you got a reason to be ashamed of her. It seems like you the one with the problem; not us. And besides, if you love her, fuck what we think."

Quan nodded his head. Suddenly, a teasing smirk crossed my face and Quan narrowed his eyes at me, knowing I was about to say some shit he might not like.

"Plus, she bad as fuck. If I didn't have Neesy, my nigga, I might swipe her super thick ass from you," I teased him.

"Man, fuck you, Leith!" Quan said with a smile. "You can't steal her from me. She loves a nigga."

"Gone head in there and handle business, nigga," Murk told him, patting him on the shoulder. "We'll see ourselves out. Big Mama in there waiting for you."

Quan knocked Murk's hand off his shoulder and glared at him.

"It ain't 'Big Mama'. Her name is Natoria."

"*Her name is NATORRRRIAAAAAA!*" we all sung out, teasing him just like they had when I'd first hooked up with Shanecia.

"Man, y'all get the fuck out of here," Quan said, but couldn't keep from laughing with us as he ushered us to the door.

Murk playfully punched him on his shoulder as Dame massaged his neck like one would do a boxer right before his toughest match. Quan batted them away with a grin on his face as we walked out his spot.

"I hate all y'all niggas. For life."

"We love yo' ass too, Quan."

Chapter Twenty-Five

SHANECIA

"I now pronounce you husband and wife," the pastor said as I stared at Maliah and Murk with tears in my eyes. "And now, I present to all of you, Mr. & Mrs. Pablo Dumas!"

We all stood on our feet and roared in celebration while clapping our hands together as Murk and Maliah kissed and walked back down the short aisle. I was so excited for her. She looked so happy and was absolutely beautiful. I'd worked overtime to make sure that she had every single thing she could ever ask for on her special day. And even though she had been acting like a bridezilla bitch with a capital 'b' the week leading up to her special day, it was all worth it now to see the smile on her face.

"You good?" Legend asked me. He ran his arm around my waist and kissed me lightly on my cheek.

Through my tears, I nodded my head as I looked at him. "I am, I'm just so happy for her."

He looked at me with a smile but I saw something hidden behind his eyes. He was thinking on something but he wasn't speaking on it yet.

"I love you," he told me and I said it right back with all sincerity.

"I love you too."

We all starting filing from out of the small church. I saw Darin and Tanecia walking ahead of me, so I sped up my pace so that I could catch up with them. Tanecia was glowing and she looked more beautiful than I'd ever seen her. The weave was out and so was the high-priced clothing. She was in a beautiful, simple, pale yellow dress and was wearing her natural hair in two-strand twists pulled into a halo style with flowers woven through it.

In her arms was the most beautiful baby I'd ever seen and I'd fallen in love with her the first time Tanecia and Darin had introduced her to me. I'd also gotten struck with baby fever, but Legend was quick to bring me to my senses by reminding me that now was not the time.

"Heyyy, little miss Jenta Amor!" I cooed as I bent down and kissed her pretty little face. She smiled back at me, showing off all of her gums.

"Tan, are you still going with me to visit mama later?" I asked her and she nodded her head.

"Yeah, I'll go. I called her last week and she told me she wanted me to sneak her some cookies," Tan replied, rolling her eyes. "They've become her new addiction."

Laughing, I nodded my head. Mama was doing pretty good so far at the rehabilitation center Legend and I put her in. She'd managed to stay clean and was gaining a lot of weight back. Mainly due to the cookies that we'd been slipping her every now and then.

"You look beautiful, Neesy," Darin said as he pulled me into a hug. "And happy."

"So do you. I guess Tan is treating you right?" I asked him with a smirk on my face as I looked at her.

"She's treating me more than right. She's treating me like a king," he replied back as he looked at her in a way that oozed true love.

"I'm the only king up in this bitch," Legend cursed from behind me. "I'm just joking with you, Darin. What's up, nigga?"

He walked up just as I grabbed Jenta up in my arms.

"Legend, don't be cursing! We're in a church!" I reprimanded him.

Chuckling, he scratched at his jaw and gave me a look.

"Well, did somebody tell Pastor Charles that?" he asked me. "I just saw him squeeze her ass on the sly."

Gasping, I turned around and looked over to where they were standing talking to each other. Maliah had told me that Aunt Loretta had a new boyfriend who she hadn't met yet, but there was no way it was the pastor she was sleeping with.

Or could it be? I thought to myself as I watched their interaction.

Aunt Loretta was smiling as they spoke to each other over in the far corner. I couldn't hear what was being said, but she seemed to definitely be enjoying every single word he was saying. Then the pastor leaned over and whispered in her ear, making her collapse into a fit of girlish giggles.

"Yeah, they fuckin," Legend confirmed from beside me.

I swatted at his arm.

"Get out the church before you get struck by lightning," I told him as Darin and Tanecia laughed.

"I may get struck but his ass is going first," Legend told me, nodding his head towards the pastor.

I rolled my eyes, planted another kiss on Jenta's pretty face and followed them all outside. It was time for the reception and I was ready to get the party started.

*****

"I'm about to leave," Maliah informed me as she walked over and kissed me on my cheek lightly, so she wouldn't mess up my makeup.

"Already?! You've only been here for an hour!" I told her as I looked her up and down.

"Right," she replied and then gave me a strange look like she was about to say something top secret. "But Murk been playing up under my dress the entire time we been sitting at the table. I'm wet as hell and ready to go!"

I burst out laughing as I looked at her while she grabbed my glass of champagne and downed it all in one gulp.

"I knew I heard a moan while Legend was saying his best man speech. Y'all some nasty muthafuckas," I teased.

"Not nastier than my damn mama," Maliah replied after she'd swallowed the liquid down. "I know she messin' with the pastor. Look at her ass! She ain't got no damn shame either. That man's wife only been dead about nine months!"

"Yeah, but it was rumored that their bedroom had been dead long before she was, if you know what I mean," I hinted with a wink. "So I'm sure he was ready to get rid of her hateful ass so he could move on to something new."

Maliah snorted out a laugh as she nodded her head. Then her eyes fell on two people laughing and talking in the opposite corner. I'd been looking at them too, and the sight of them surprised me in some ways but not in others.

"So Cush and Alani. Are they...?" Maliah let her voice trail off but she gave me a look that told me exactly what she was trying to ask.

I let my eyes return to where Cush and Alani were talking in hushed tones in the corner, much in the same way that Aunt Loretta had been doing with the pastor. In the same fashion, Alani bent down and whispered in Cush's ear. Sweet nothings. Cush giggled her glee. She looked girlish and innocent. Neither one of them had a single care in the world.

"I think they are," I said finally. "Cush told me that she had something she wasn't sure she wanted to tell her brothers just yet. I'm thinking this is it. She...likes girls."

"Oh, I think her brothers already know," Maliah laughed and pointed to the other side.

Murk, Quan, Dame, and Legend were all standing around with drinks in their hands talking about something that obviously had to do with Cush because they were looking right at her. She was just so caught up by Alani, she hadn't even noticed.

"Yeah they do," I said with a smile as I watched Legend. "She might as well come on out of that closet."

LEGEND

"So Cush is *gay*?" Quan asked as he looked over at where our sister sat chatting with Trell's sister, Alani.

"She's a lesbian," Dame told him.

"So she's a *gay lesbian*?" Quan inquired with his brows knotted in confusion.

"Nigga, shut yo' dumb ass up!" Murk replied, jabbing Quan in the ribs.

"I knew it the whole while," Dame told us with a pompous look on his face. "Trell said that she told her but she made her promise to keep it secret."

"But she told your dumb ass?" Murk asked with one brow lifted.

Dame sipped from his cup and then shrugged. "We promised we weren't keeping no more secrets from each other."

"How much we know about this Alani chick?" Quan questioned as he ran his fingers along his beard. "Nigga or not, she fuck with Cush's heart, I'mma drop her ass."

"Alani cool peoples," Dame told us. "Y'all know that shit. But you right, she fuck up and she can get it."

I watched Cush as she laughed and flirted with Alani and it made me smile, but it also made me feel some kind of way. Both she and Quan had hid from me the person who they loved. Why? Was I that hard to speak to? Was my family afraid of me? I knew they respected me but I never wanted that respect to turn into terror.

At that very moment, Cush turned and glanced in my direction, her eyes locking on mine. I saw a bit of apprehension pass through them and it hurt my heart that she would feel that way; scared that I wouldn't accept her because of her choice when it came to love.

Smiling, I lifted my glass to her in cheers and nodded my head to let her know that she had my blessings. Her smile grew wide on her face, almost completely taking it over. She blew me a kiss and then bowed her head in thanks. I felt the heat of someone's eyes on me and when I turned to my right, I saw Shanecia looking at me, her eyes filled with tears. She was so damn emotional tonight. Every little thing was making her cry. I loved her emotional ass but she needed to get her hormones in check. I needed to make sure her crybaby ass wasn't pregnant.

"Hold my glass before I lose my nerve," I heard Dame suddenly say and before I could react, he thrust his glass into my hand and began to walk away.

"What is his ass up to?" Murk asked.

I shrugged and watched him as he walked up to the DJ booth, grabbed the mic and then stepped back out onto the middle of the floor.

"EVERYBODY HUSH RIGHT NOW! I got something I need to say!" he announced to the crowd.

All the chatter died down as we waited to see what it was that he had to say.

"Trell, can you come out here, please?"

Along with everyone else, I watched in silence as Trell left from where she'd been chatting with Quan's girl, Natoria, and walked hesitantly towards Dame.

"Oh shit!" Quan jeered as we all saw Dame take her hand and drop to one knee.

I felt a thump in my chest and I turned to look at Shanecia. She had tears in her eyes again and her hands were up to her mouth.

Shit, I thought to myself as I fumbled with something inside my pocket. Looking over at Murk, I saw that he was staring right back at me. He shrugged and then we both turned to Dame and Trell.

"Trell, I don't have no long ass speech or nothing," he continued. "But I do want to let you know that leaving me was the best thing you've ever done, but I can't take that shit if you leave my sorry ass again. I need you…you're the only woman I'll ever want and ever need. Will you please marry me?"

"YES!!!!" Trell screamed as she jumped up and down. Dame jumped up off his knees, scooped her up in his arms and swirled her around as everyone clapped and hooted in celebration.

"Gone head and make it do what it do, nigga," Murk taunted me while giving me a light push on the arm. "You already late as hell as it is."

"Fuck outta here, man," I laughed and walked away towards Shanecia. I caught her eye and motioned for her to follow me outside.

"Hey baby," I said as I grabbed her hand once we were outside.

She gave me a small smile that didn't quite reach her eyes and I knew what the reason was. Shanecia didn't have to say a thing for me to know what was going on in her head. I could feel it in my soul when she wasn't right. And I could feel it in my soul when she was. Every emotion…every feeling that had to do with her was in me.

"Why you got that sourpuss ass look on your face?" I asked with a smirk, knowing I was about to get on her nerves.

"Legend…I'm just tired, that's all," she said with a sigh as she rolled her eyes.

Pausing for a beat, I looked up at the night sky and admired how beautiful everything around us looked. We were outside the reception hall that Maliah had picked for the wedding reception. It was grand as fuck and big as hell, which was insane to me because there was only about twenty-five of us invited to the wedding but Maliah wanted it so Murk gave it to her. It was nice though…and the perfect setting for what I wanted to do.

"Your ass always tired. You sure you ain't pregnant or some shit?" I queried with a raised brow as I jabbed her in her stomach. "You seem like you might be getting a lil' thick in the ass. When the last time yo' period came on?"

"Stop fuckin' with me, Legend," she scoffed, rolling her eyes and sucking her teeth. "You know I'm not pregnant. You make sure of that."

I grabbed her hand but she snatched away from me. I snatched her ass right back and held her tight.

"Don't be snatching away from me, nigga," I told her playfully. She frowned but I saw the smile inching up on the side of her face.

"Legend, stop playing all the damn time!" she laughed and

pushed me away. I stepped back and bit my lip. It was either now or never. The time was now.

So that was when I did it.

Under the cloak of night while looking at the most beautiful woman I'd ever laid eyes on, I dropped to one knee. Shanecia gasped loud as hell and once again placed her hands to her open mouth as she watched me.

Shit, I thought. *The fuck am I wanting to say?*

There was a lot of shit I'd had in mind to tell her but I'd lost it all. My heart was beating a mile a minute and I was nervous as fuck. Here I was giving my heart to a woman and asking her if she would be mine… forever. Would she say no? If she did, I knew I was going to pull out my strap and light this bitch up like the Fourth of July. I couldn't take it if Shanecia refused to be mine.

"Shanecia…"

"YESSS!" she yelled out as she jumped up and down with her hands in the air and tears running down her face.

"Shit, man, let me get it out first!" I laughed as I watched her. She calmed down a little and I started to speak.

"Shanecia, I loved you since the first day I met you," I started. "Maybe not right *when* I met you but after I had time to think about what you did, I knew that I loved you. You risked your life for someone you loved and that's what I've always been about. No one on this Earth has ever made me feel like I was truly invincible…like I didn't have to prove myself to them. No one but you.

When I look into your eyes, I see everything that I need. You're my rib. You're the missing piece of me that I never knew I needed. I can't let you go… not now and not ever."

I felt myself start to get choked up so I paused to get myself together. This shit was intense. I never knew it would be like this.

"All them books I been sneaking and reading from your tablet always have these men in them who always say the right thing. And I wish they would toss a hint to my ass right now because I can't think of any of that sweet shit right now, but I just want you to know that I love you and I always will. You're my whole life. Will you please do me the honor of promising to be with me, be the mother my children, and give me hope of better days for the rest of my life…will you please marry me?"

With tears in her eyes, Shanecia just silently looked at me as if stunned. My heart throbbed in my chest as I waited her to say something…anything. What the hell was going on?

"Nigga, say something—"

"YES!!" she shouted again. "Of course, I'll marry you!"

Taking a deep breath of relief, I placed the ring on her finger and stood up. As soon as I did she wrapped her arms around me and jumped right on me, lassoing her legs around my waist. I planted kiss after kiss on her face as she cried in my arms. She was happy. I was stricken with disbelief that this moment had actually arrive. I was about to be a married man to the perfect woman. Everything was perfect.

Until it wasn't.

Just as I put her down, ten black cars swerved into the parking lot, surrounding us, followed by two large black vans. Before I could move to grab my piece, uniformed officers jumped out of the vehicles in SWAT team gear, complete with AKs, shotguns and bulletproof vests. Shanecia screamed and placed her hands in the air as they pointed their weapons on us. I gritted my teeth as my eyes danced back and forth and my mind calculated the various outcomes to this new situation. None of them were good.

"FREEZE! Put your hands in the air!" one of the officers shouted over the loud speaker as we looked on. I looked at the letters on the jackets of all of the white faces in front of me. It was the FBI.

A blaring white light turned on right in my face, blinding me. I heard movement behind me and knew it was probably my brothers filing out of the church.

Just then, a tall, black woman walked up to me with three agents to her side.

Oh shit, I thought as I looked at the letters on her jacket. *Fuckin'* FBI. I already had a feeling of what this was about.

I turned to look behind me and saw Murk, Dame, and Quan behind me with stoic, unreadable expressions on their faces. They weren't saying a word but their eyes were moving back and forth as they took in the scene. I knew they were thinking the same thing I was.

"Leith, Pablo, and Damion Dumas?" the female agent said as she looked back and forth between us.

We didn't say a word.

"You don't have to say anything," she replied with a sigh. "I already know who you are. Let's take them in."

253

"What da fuck do you want with us?!" Dame yelled out as the agents came on us, latching handcuffs on each of our wrists.

"Leith Dumas, Pablo Dumas, and Damion Dumas, you are all under arrest for the murder of a federal agent. You have the right to remain silent. Anything you say or do…"

Clenching my jaw, I squeezed my eyes shut before swooping them over to Shanecia's face. She looked utterly devastated as she wiped at her tear-filled eyes with the hand that held the ring I'd just placed there. On the day that was supposed to be the happiest, she was crying tears of sheer terror after hearing that I'd been arrested for killing a federal agent. This was far from good.

With tears in her eyes, Maliah ran out of the church and wrapped Shanecia in her arms and they cried together as the agents carted us all away. I couldn't even say anything as the agents handcuffed us all and roughly led us to one of the black vans to take us off to jail. The only thing that kept cycling in my mind was that I'd fucked up.

Again.

The more I tried to get things right, the more it seemed things were going wrong; spiraling completely out of my control. I'd gotten rid of all of my enemies and ensured Shanecia's safety but, in doing so, I'd opened her up to another situation that I wasn't sure she was prepared for.

Life without me

TO BE CONTINUED

NOTE FROM PORSCHA STERLING

Thank you for reading!

I really enjoy reading about these characters and I hope you love them as much as I do. I did plan on ending this at book 3 BUT I have so many more issues that I want to explore and some of the other couples need time to speak about their struggles.

Cush and Alani...did you see that coming? I'll be honest and say I didn't! Dame and Trell are now together and ENGAGED but I'm sure, as with any relationship plagued by infidelities and lack of trust, they will have issues of their own to face!

Were you surprised or shocked that Quan finally found love? His lil' stingy, joking self needed someone special in his life. And, remember, her name is NATORRRIAAAAA!

What is up with Ms. Loretta and the pastor?! Saved folks got some drama, don't they? The pastor has her slipping in some new reading material inside her Bible and all. Isn't that just a mess?!

Legend and Shanecia...can they catch a break? Legend has some tough decisions to make...if he can make it out of this last situation. He's grown so much over such a short time and Shanecia has been the impetus for that. But after being faced with this new dilemma, what will she decide to do? Legend definitely needs her right now and I hope she pulls through to be the one he needs.

Maliah and Murk are going through what no couple has to. To be pregnant with twins and have your fiancé arrested only hours after you've said your vows is a terrible predicament to be in. But if we know anything about Maliah, it's that she is TOUGH and sister-girl is no stranger to STANDING BY HER MAN!

Get ready because PART FOUR IS COMING SOON!

Please make sure to leave a review! I love reading them!

I would love it if you reach out to me on Facebook, Instagram or Twitter!

Also, join my Facebook group! I love to interact with my readers. If you haven't already, text PORSCHA to 25827 to join my text list. Text ROYALTY to 42828 to join our email list and read excerpts and learn about giveaways.

Peace, love & blessings to everyone. I love allllll of you!

Porscha Sterling

MAKE SURE TO LEAVE A REVIEW!

Text PORSCHA to 25827
to keep up with Porscha's latest releases!

To find out more about her, visit www.porschasterling.com

Join our mailing list to get a notification when Leo Sullivan Presents has another release!

Text **LEOSULLIVAN** to **22828** to join!

To submit a manuscript for our review, email us at leosullivanpresents@gmail.com